Little Charlie

By

James L. McKinney

@Easy Reading Books

Copyright 2018

Little Charlie

After letting the horses drink from the shallow basin, Jasper led them to the rear of the enclosure and tied them. His dark eyes fastened on Charlie as he turned and spoke to Lloyd. "That supper shor' smells good. I'm half starved. The kid ain't give you no trouble today, has he?"

"None a'tall, Jasper." He glanced quickly at Charlie. "He's been quiet as a mouse at a Sunday meeting."

"Too bad." He grinned wolfishly at Charlie as he stepped closer. "I was hoping I'd have reason to plug him. Kids always did get on my nerves. I never did like 'em."

Little Charlie

Chapter One

Charlie stood on his tiptoes with the box underneath his feet tottering dangerously and lifted the box of nails a little higher. "Just a little bit more," he breathed nervously to himself as he stretched his small arms to their full length.

Suddenly the heavy box tilted sideways and he lost his grip on the nails. Becoming unbalanced on the box he was standing on he reached out with his left hand and seized the top of the shelf.

The box of nails slipped from his hand and landed with a loud crash. He frantically clawed at the top of the shelf with his right hand to keep from falling. The box beneath his feet turned over and he was left swinging to the top of the tall shelf.

His weight was too much for the shelf and

it lurched toward the floor lurched toward the floor.

Bert Godwin, proprietor of the hardware store rushed into the storeroom at the sound of the crashing box of nails. He was just in time to see Charlie swing himself free from the tall shelf of goods and, with a jumping roll of his body barely escape the shelf as it crashed to the floor, splattering its contents in every direction.

Bert's face reddened with anger and his beetle brows narrowed. He quickly grabbed a broom setting beside the door. "Charlie Matthews! You good-for-nothing little red-headed coyote! Look what you've done." He swung the broom violently toward Charlie's head.

Charlie ducked the sweeping blow and scrambled to his feet. His nerves were still rattled by his narrow escape of death. He darted behind the large bolts of cloth.

Charlie was just a little fellow with an unruly shock of red hair. His nose and cheeks were covered with bright freckles. In all of his thirteen years he had managed to stretch his height to only five feet and three inches and his weight to one hundred and ten pounds. Perhaps he could have weighed more but he could never seem to get enough to eat.

As he peered over the huge bolts of cloth at Mr. Godwin he was sure that he wouldn't be eating again this evening.

It seemed like everything he touched got broken and what didn't break got torn up in some other way. Things just had a way of falling apart around him.

"It wasn't my fault that dad-jim box gave way under my feet!" His eyes brightened as Bert advanced upon him slowly with the broom lifted high for another blow. "I's darn lucky I wasn't killed!"

"You may have escaped death once but sure aren't gonna escape me, you little weasel. It will take me most of the night to clean up this mess you've made. Not only are you fired but I'm gonna whale the daylights out of you."

"You hit me with that broom, Mr. Godwin and I'll kick the fire outa you. I'm a warning you!" As Charlie spoke the freckles on his face turned darker and his light blue eyes grew even lighter until they appeared to be clear.

"Sassing me too, are you? Well, I'll teach you some manners. It's time someone did so I'm gonna start the lessons now." He swung the broom back over his shoulder and edged a little closer toward Charlie.

Charlie knew he was in trouble and was

preparing his defenses when the body of Mrs. Godwin filled the doorway. Her voice was sharp and commanding. "Bert Godwin! What in heaven's name are you doing? You might hurt Charlie with that broom."

"Get out of here, Elsie! I warned you what would happen if we hired this little lunatic! Look at what he's done. He's torn the place apart!"

Elsie's eyes narrowed. "How dare you raise your voice to me, Bert Godwin!" She picked up a broom from the rack near her and began closing in on her husband. She was buxom woman and fearless as a tigriss.

A slight grin touched Charlie's lips as he saw what was coming. He took a step out from the cloth and as he did Bert started to swing the broom.

Bert never completed the crippling blow for a sharp whap on his backside from Mrs. Godwin prevented the fatal blow.

"You have customers waiting, Mr. Godwin," she said sharply. "I would suggest that you attend to them and leave off this ridiculous foolin' around." She glanced at Charlie. "Come here, Charlie."

As Charlie stepped slowly and cautiously toward her he began to apologize. "I'm sorry,

Mrs. Godwin. I didn't mean to cause any trouble. Mr. Godwin sure got upset, didn't he?"

Elsie's eyes were filled with tenderness as she looked at Charlie and thought about his difficult situation which fate had placed upon him. "You leave Mr. Godwin to me. Are you okay?"

"I'm fine now. Do you want me to start cleaning up this mess I made?"

"No, Charlie. I'll attend to it later." She reached into her pocket and extracted a silver coin. "Here, take this."

Charlie took the silver dollar in his small hand as a crooked grin formed at the corners of his mouth. "Much obliged, Mrs. Godwin."

"You best disappear before Bert gets back in here. No telling what he may try to do to you the next time."

"I'll be seeing you then." He turned and quickly disappeared out the back door.

As Charlie emerged on the back street he drew the soft, rawhide strap a little tighter around his waist. He had been waiting longingly for suppertime. It seemed he always got fired just before meal time. After fondling the silver dollar in his hand for a few seconds he pushed it into his back pocket. He wondered where he might be able to land another job. For him they were getting scarce as hen's teeth. Mr. Godwin's hardware store had been his last good prospect and now it too was gone.

Since he had fouled up at the sheriff's office and let two prisoners escape he had been barred from ever going near the place again. Sheriff Metters' last words still echoed loudly in his mind. "If I ever catch you near the place again I'll lock you up."

His job of swamping the saloon had also ended in disaster. A ruckus had broken out over him in the Silver Spur and Con Silvers, the owner had literally taken a shot at him as he ducked out the back door.

He couldn't return to the stables for Dobbs had threatened his life when he accidentally knocked over a lantern and caught the place on fire.

The only two friends he had were Mrs. Godwin and Maria Costella who ran Maria's Boarding House. He would have to approach her again tonight for any supper leftovers.

He would go stay with his big brother Tom but he had been prohibited from ever getting around him again. The last time he had seen him was a year ago when he had ridden out to his camp.

Tom was a big man, standing six feet and

two inches and weighing close to two hundred pounds. Looking at his brown, curly hair and light green eyes no one would have ever dreamed that he and Charlie were brothers. He lived on the shady side of the law and forbade Charlie from ever entering his camp again.

Perhaps he could ride out to the Rocking D and enquire after a job. The talk was going around that the ranch was being hit hard by rustlers and the Drakes were in danger of losing it. Major Ben Colter of the Bar C had been trying to buy them out but they kept refusing his offers.

He headed for the small corral behind the blacksmith shop. He had reached a decision. He would ride out to the Rocking D. If he hurried he may get there in time for chuck.

After saddling the small, shaggy mustang Charlie leaped into the saddle. As he rode up the dusty street there were at least a dozen pair of eyes watching his departure. Among them was Bert Godwin who was standing at the window. As he stared at Charlie his eyes grew hard and mean. He looked again at the double-barrel shotgun standing in the rack near his side. It was a longing, tempting look that he gave the gun.

Charlie picked up his pace to a shambling trot as he took the south trail out of Three Forks.

He liked the sound of Running Water Creek that ran parallel to the trail. Bearing east, it gave life to the Rocking D ranch. That was the real reason that Major Ben Colter wanted the ranch. With the Rocking D in his possession he could enlarge his herds by a few thousand and have one of the largest ranches in western Texas.

He had covered about seven miles when he saw the saddled horse standing by the trail with its reins trailing the ground. It was a beautiful chestnut mare with a blaze face.

He slowed his mustang as he drew nearer and looked cautiously around. He could hear the waters of the creek gulping and fussing around the rocks as they flowed through the still, warm afternoon.

He halted his horse about ten yards from the mare and dismounted. Advancing on foot toward the mare he began speaking in a low, assuring tone. After getting hold of the reins he tied them to a tree branch and began searching the immediate area.

His eyes fell on the body that was lying in the grass that grew near the edge of the creek. It was a woman and by the looks of her light blue shirt she had been hurt. The side and part of the front were stained with blood.

He rushed to her side and turned her face

upward for a look. His eyes widened as he recognized her. It was Bonnie Drake of the Rocking D and she had been shot.

He tore his kerchief loose from his neck and dipped it into the cold waters of the creek. She moved slightly as he sponged her pale face.

Again he soaked the kerchief. This time he held it above her partly open lips and let a few trickles run into her mouth. It brought an immediate response.

After a few short, strangled coughs she blinked open her eyes. "Oh-ooo," she whispered hoarsely, gritting her teeth against the pain in her side. She looked up into the face of Charlie who was bending over her. There was a faint quiver in her voice as she spoke. "Where, uh, where am I? What happened?"

"Easy, Mrs. Drake. Lie still, you hear? You've been shot. I was passing by and found you here. I'm Charlie Matthews."

"Charlie Matthews? Of Three Forks?"

"Yes, ma'am, Charlie Matthews of Three Forks. You just lie still now and we'll get that wound cleaned and bandaged. I'll ride with you on to the ranch."

After the wound had been washed and bandaged, Bonnie stood to her feet with unsteady movements. She was still a bit dizzy but her head had cleared.

"Any idea who shot you, Mrs. Drake? I mean, did you see anyone?"

"Not a soul, Charlie. The shot seemed to have come from that ridge up there. Rustlers have been stealing us blind but I can't imagine who would want to murder me."

"Well, if you're able to ride, ma'am, maybe you should ride into town and let Doc Sweezy have a look at your side."

"Perhaps that would be best. Thank you for helping me. Where did you say you were heading when you found me?"

"I was riding out to see you. I'm looking for a job."

"I only have two hands left at the ranch, Charlie. The rustlers have spooked the others and they left. Only Weber and Crowley stayed. I'm afraid they'll be killed. I hardly know what to do. The sheriff never seems to have any luck finding the rustlers of my cattle. I may be forced to sell out to Major Colter."

Charlie and Bonnie dismounted at the doctor's office and stepped inside.

Doctor Sweezy fixed hard eyes on Charlie as he looked at Bonnie's side. "You wasn't involved in this, was you young man?"

"Oh no, Doctor Sweezy," cut in Bonnie

quickly. "Charlie is the one who found me. I don't know what may have happened to me if he hadn't come along."

As the doctor worked over Bonnie's wound the door opened and Sheriff Bob Metters stepped inside. He glanced from Bonnie to Charlie. "Saw you ride in, Mrs. Drake. Are you okay?"

"I'll be fine, sheriff, thanks to Charlie."

"What happened?"

"Some low-down coyote shot her," said Charlie harshly.

Metters cast a mean glance at Charlie. "I'm speaking to Mrs. Drake, boy." He focused his attention back to Bonnie. "Any idea who shot you? I'll ride out and take a look around." He shifted suspicious eyes at Charlie.

"Not at all. I was returning home when the bullet hit me and knocked me from my saddle. I saw no one."

"I tried to catch you before you left town. Wanted to give you this." He reached her a piece of paper. "It's a telegram from Amarillo. If you need me I'll be close around." After giving Charlie another mean eye he stepped outside.

Bonnie paid the doctor and with Charlie following, they rode out of town on her way home.

"As I was saying earlier, Charlie, working for me could be very dangerous. Whoever shot me may try again and they may try to kill you too."

"I'll be okay, Ms. Drake. I'm a light sleeper and I can help watch the ranch for you."

Bonnie remembered the telegram and pulled it from her pocket. She unfolded it and began reading.

Charlie saw her face turn ashen and tears fill her eyes as she read the message.

She pulled the mare to a halt and sat still in the saddle, staring silently out over the plains that stretched away to the south. Suddenly as if coming out of a trance she turned quickly to Charlie. "I'm sorry. I just forgot myself there for a moment."

Unable to constrain herself she broke out in a low, sobbing cry. "I don't know what I'm gonna do now. The telegram was from the sheriff in Amarillo. It was about Luke. He was killed in a gunfight by some passing stranger by the name of Tom. He'd been drinking heavy again and spoiling for a fight. They released the man who killed him."

"I sure am sorry, Ms. Drake. I didn't know your husband very well but I liked him."

"I'm going to fight to hold the ranch as long as I can. I don't know how long that will be, Charlie."

Charlie's eyes brightened and his voice was filled with excitement. "That's the spirit, Ms. Drake. I'll help you too! If you've got an extra gun at the ranch I reckon I better start toting one. We'll give them two-bit rustlers a run for their money."

Bonnie reached out her hand to Charlie and smiled. "We'll shake on that, Charlie. Let's ride now."

Little Charlie

Chapter Two

Major Ben Colter rode down the street of Three Forks like a soldier on a parade ground. This was his town and as soon as he acquired the Rocking D ranch he would own everything in two hundred square miles including Sheriff Metters.

He halted his horse and dismounted in front of the Silver Spur. He was dressed to perfection in his blue-grey uniform that was spotless. With his head held high and his back straight as an arrow he stepped inside the saloon.

Following closely on his heels were his two lieutenants, Shep Gorman and Stu Biggers. They were gunmen who hailed from Wichita Falls, deep in the Indian Territory. Being an eye witness to an exhibition of their gun work five years previous, Colter had immediately taken them into his employment.

Shep was a short, stocky man with wide, powerful shoulders and exceedingly long arms. He boasted of having broken at least one man's back with them and as far as rough and tumble brawls he had never been beaten. His head was set on a short, thick neck.

Stu was just the opposite in his physical make-up. He was tall, slim, and his pointed head set on a long, narrow neck. His long, hawk-billed nose and deep set eyes gave him the appearance of a great bird. He wore large-roweled, California spurs on his boots that rattled loudly when he walked. Where Shep was grumpy and short tempered, Stu was easy-going, good-natured and long on patience. When the limits of his patience was reached however, he became a dangerous man, or as some had said of him, a killing machine. Twelve men down his back trail could testify to his quickness with the forty-five he carried low on his hip and tied down. That is… if they were alive and could talk.

"Howdy, Major," spoke Con Silvers from behind the bar. "What can I get you?"

"Three whiskeys, Con." He turned his back to the bar and looked over the loungers at the tables. When he saw the sheriff and another man sitting at a table he headed their way with his drink in his hand. "Howdy, sheriff, Dave. Mind if I join you?"

"Have a seat, Major," spoke Metters quickly. "I was just fixing to call for you. I guess you heard about Ms. Drake?"

"Nothing lately, except she's missing some cattle. She must not have many left. Someone passed the word that she's lost better than a thousand head." He scooted back a chair and sat down. "Nothing new has come up, has it?"

"She was shot yesterday on her way home. Little Charlie found her out near the creek and brought her in. Luke was killed in Amarillo. Kinda puts her in a bind, I'd say."

Colter took a swallow of his drink. "Perhaps I should ride out and see her again. She may be ready to sell now."

The three men pulled themselves closer to the table and lowered their voices.

Colter fixed hard, piercing eyes on Dave. "What's the word from Tom?"

"He said to tell you he had nigh on to twelve hundred head holed up in Red Fox Canyon. He and his men want to make a drive soon. Said it was too risky to hold the cattle much longer."

"You take him word to hold them a little longer. I think Ms. Drake may be ready to sell any day now. She's only got a couple of hands left." He reached into his pocket and extracted a thin sheaf of bills. He counted out a hundred dollars and handed it to Dave. "Take Tom a couple of bottles and tell him I'll get word back to him real soon as to when he can move the cattle."

Dave stood to his feet and stared at the money with a wide smile. "I'll be leaving now."

Colter waited until Dave had stepped out of hearing and lowered his voice to hardly more than a whisper. "No use losing all those cattle. As soon as I get the Rocking D you can wind things up by calling in the U.S. Marshal and letting him round up the rustlers. With someone to point out their camp to him he shouldn't have any trouble."

A slight frown crossed Metters' face. "You sure you want to double-cross Tom? He can get mighty ugly when his dander is raised."

"If he finds out I'll turn Shep and Stu loose on him. Besides, if the marshal catches him he won't be bothering anyone for a long, long time." He pushed back his chair and stood to his feet as he finished off his drink. "I'm riding on out. I think I'll drop by and have another chat with Ms. Drake." He set his glass on the table and motioned for Shep and Stu to follow as he walked out of the saloon.

The trio mounted their horses and rode out of town on the south trail following along Running Water Creek.

Two hours later they pulled into the yard of the Rocking D. The place looked to be empty but they could hear the ring of an axe somewhere behind the house.

Colter dismounted and stepped to the door. As he knocked, Shep and Stu took their positions on the porch.

His knock was answered by the opening of the door and the soft voice of Bonnie. "Mr. Colter? Won't you come in?"

"Much obliged, Ms. Drake." He took off his hat and stepped inside. As he looked around the front room his eyes filled with admiration of the woman's touch of cleanliness. The room was arranged neatly. Not only was this widow woman as good as any cowhand out on the range but she knew how to keep a house. "I heard about Luke from the sheriff. Sorry you lost your husband, Ms. Drake. Anything I can do for you?"

"No thanks. I don't guess there is much

anyone can do, that is, unless you could catch those rustlers who are stealing me blind."

"I've had my men out looking. Been out a couple of times myself. We followed their tracks over toward the northbound trail. Most of the cattlemen are honest men although now and then one might take a small herd if the price was right."

"Well, they won't be rustling many more. I only have about seven hundred head left. Weber and Crowley moved them in closer to the house and we're keeping a careful eye on them. If the rustlers should get them it will put me under."

"I'll give you a fair price for the ranch. I don't like to see anyone come on to hard times like you have."

"No, I'm going to hold off selling as long as I can. Hopefully there will be a turning of the tide soon. Thanks for your concern but I'm not ready to sell yet."

"Whatever you say. If I can be of any help in the meanwhile, you just send one of your men for me."

"Thank you so much. I take that very neighborly."

Colter walked to the door to leave. "I'll be riding then. So long, Ms. Drake."

"Thanks again for everything, Major."

Colter's eyes were hard as he mounted his horse and rode from the yard. He waited until he and his men were out of hearing of the house, then spoke sharply to Shep and Stu. "Get six or seven of the men ready tonight. While two men with rifles keep the house busy the rest of you can stampede those cattle. Run 'em south. We can get word to Tom to pick them up."

"Sure, boss," answered Stu with his long drawl. "I guess that will about break her back, uh?"

"She'll be begging me to buy her ranch in a few days."

Weber and Crowley had agreed to take turns guarding the herd that were bunched a half mile from the house. As Crowley rode off for the first watch, Weber headed for the bunkhouse.

The stars were out and the night was still, broken only by a faint breeze that moved softly and started the dark shadows to dancing in the moonlight.

Charlie walked through the ranch yard taking a last look around the house before retiring for the night. Satisfied that all was well he headed for the bunkhouse. He stopped suddenly as the silence was broken by gunfire.

He saw the bullets striking the doors of the house and bunkhouse.

He hit the ground hard, rolling under the wagon which had been left in the yard. Hunkering down behind the wagon wheel he strained his eyes for sign of the attackers.

He saw the rifle fire coming from the low ridge above the house. By the muzzle fire he decided there were two of them. So far, he doubted that they knew his location for no bullets were hitting near him.

He waited until Weber began returning fire from the bunkhouse and darted for the corner of the corral. Behind the bars he moved slowly and cautiously toward the big cottonwood that was twenty paces away. From there he could sneak around behind the men on the hilltop.

He waited until the rifles began cracking again and dashed for the tree. He made it unseen.

A half dozen guns opened up in the direction of the cattle and blending in with the gunfire and stampeding cattle he heard the high-pitched scream of a man in agony. It lasted for only a few seconds and was drowned out by the pounding hooves of the cattle.

Charlie dashed from the tree and made it to the base of the ridge. He ascended the hillside quickly and lowered himself into a shallow hollow. He lifted his head and peered at the spot where the riflemen were concealed. They were only forty yards from where he lay. Pulling the heavy forty-four from his belt, he eared back the hammer. Taking careful aim, he fired.

A yelp of pain sounded as one of the men threw up his arms and rolled over in the grass.

Startled by the attack from the side and rear, the second man turned quickly and fired two rapid shots in Charlie's direction.

Charlie fired again and, peering over the edge of the hollow he saw the man hunkered down and moving silently away. The gun leaped in his hands and he saw the man's arm jerk violently, causing him to lose hold on his rifle.

The man leaped down the hillside, lost his footing and began rolling. He rolled out of Charlie's sight.

Charlie waited for what must have been ten seconds. Deciding the ambusher had left for good, he stood to his feet and listened. After a long minute he heard the hoof beats of a racing horse moving away in the darkness.

Without taking time to check on the man that he saw roll over in the grass he raced back down the hill toward the house. He was met in the yard by Weber.

Weber's eyes were wide with shock as he looked at the forty-four still clutched in Charlie's hand. "Was that you rootin' out those fellows on the ridge, Charlie?"

"Yeah, I got one of them or at least I winged him. He was still lying on the ground when I left. I hurried back to check on you and Bonnie and I didn't take time to see if he was dead or not."

"Everything's okay here. Ms. Drake is shook up some but not hurt. Mighty brave thing you did. The bad part of it is, they got the rest of the cattle.

Crowley's not come in either. They may have killed him."

"I reckon I better ride out and check on him. You can stay with Ms. Drake." Charlie roped his mustang and, after saddling it, headed out to look for Crowley.

A half hour later he found the mangled remains of the body. It had been churned into the ground by the pounding hooves of the cattle. He turned his head from the nauseating sight and rode back toward the house. He would return with a ground sheet and gather the remains of the body for burial.

Sheriff Metters sipped slowly on his coffee as he sat listening to Bonnie's recap of the previous night's attack on the ranch and the death of Crowley.

"When Weber and Charlie went back up on the ridge top this morning the body of the man was gone. There was plenty of blood on the grass but we don't really know if the man was killed or not. If he was dead someone returned during the night for his body."

Sheriff Metters shook his head negatively. "I wish someone had seen a face or something. Undoubtedly it was the same bunch who've been doing all the rustling. I'll keep looking. Hopefully something will turn up soon." He stood up and picked up his hat to leave. "I'll keep check with you in case I turn up anything." He stepped outside.

Bonnie remained at the table in silence, her head laid upon her folded arms. Her mind was a troubled mass of despair. Her cattle were gone. Luke was dead. Only Weber and little Charlie were left to stand with her.

Defeated and broken, she began to weep lowly. At the sound of the door opening she lifted her head as Charlie appeared in the doorway.

"I hope I'm not bothering you, Ms. Drake.

Little Charlie

It's just that I've been wondering about what you intend to do now. You want Weber and me to follow those cattle tracks?"

"There's no use to, Charlie. Even if you caught up with them you would only be killed. I guess the only thing left for me to do is sell out to Major Colter."

Charlie dropped his head and began nervously fondling the tattered hat in his hands. "I've got something on my mind, Ms. Drake. I can't tell you all about it right now but before you let the ranch go I'd like for you to give me a few days to work on it. I think I may know how to save your ranch."

Bonnie stared at him through tender, tear-filled eyes. "Oh, Charlie, can't you see? There's no way! I've thought of everything."

"I think maybe there is a way. Like I was saying, I'll need a few days. I'll have a bit of riding to do. Will you give me your word that you'll hold off a few more days?"

"Why certainly, if you insist. This plan of yours isn't going to get you into trouble, is it?"

Charlie stepped nearer the table. "I can't rightly say what might happen. All I can tell you is that I'll be back in a few days. I wouldn't want any of this conversation repeated though. It will be our secret, okay?"

Bonnie looked curiously at him and again her eyes misted over. "Not a solitary person shall hear of it. It will be our secret."

"Much obliged, Ms. Drake. I reckon I best be riding now. You take care until I return." He turned to leave.

"You be careful, Charlie. I don't know what we would have done without you last night. Weber said you probably saved our lives. And Charlie… there's something else."

Charlie turned to face her. "Yes?"

"You may call me Bonnie from now on. We are friends, aren't we?"

Charlie's eyes brightened and grew wider. "You bet, Bonnie. I'll see you in a few days." He quickly turned and walked out of the room.

Little Charlie

Chapter Three

Charlie rode on under the hot, shimmering rays of the sun into the afternoon with occasional glances at the cattle tracks stretching out before him. In the distance ahead he could see the towering mesas that were split with canyons. All afternoon he kept pushing the tired, shaggy mustang, stopping only long enough to refill his canteen and let the horse quench its thirst.

As he lifted his eyes and glanced morosely at the brassy sky his thoughts ran ahead to his planned destination.

Tom's camp was located in the back of a canyon whose steep sides reached upward toward the clouds. There was a secret exit but it was known only to Tom and his men. He wondered what his big brother would say when he rode into his camp.

As he watched the strange whirling of the dust devils playing and dancing ahead, his attention was suddenly drawn on farther down the trail. There was a large dust cloud evidently made by a large herd of cattle or horses.

He glanced at the sky again. It was getting on up in the evening and time for travelers to start looking for a campsite. If the dust cloud in the distance was being made by white men they would be stopping soon. It wasn't far to Tom's camp and he wondered if it could be him and his men ahead. With the tracks of the cattle leading ahead he pushed wearily on.

He heard the swishing of the rope but it settled around his arms and body before he had time to move. He was jerked from the saddle and hit the hot sand hard. His head was rattled from the impact.

Two men stepped from behind the large rocks by the trail. They were grinning as they walked nearer, keeping their eyes fixed on Charlie.

It was the one holding the rope that spoke. "Look at what we got here, Tap. Doggone if it don't resemble a boy."

"Can't be much of one, Jed, judging by the

looks of that flea-bitten mustang. It ain't much bigger than a shaggy dog."

"What are you doing out here in the middle of nowhere, boy?" spoke the one called Tap.

"Hunting," answered Charlie as he tried to free himself from the rope. "You oughta be more careful what you're dabbing your rope on, mister! You purty nigh broke my neck!" He began rubbing his arms and elbows.

Jed burst out laughing. "Did you hear that, Tap? He's liable to give us a thrashing any minute now." His voice suddenly took on a more serious tone. "Just what are you hunting, boy, besides scorpions and rattlesnakes? This sure ain't hunting country."

"I'm hunting a man. His name is Tom." He stood to his feet and threw the rope on the ground.

"Tom, you say. Has this here Tom got a last name?"

"Yeah, he's got a last name but it don't matter none what it is."

Tap studied the red head and the layer of bright freckles on Charlie's face suspiciously as if he was trying to bring something or someone to his remembrance. As Charlie bent over to retrieve his hat, it hit him. The alarm filled his eyes and showed in the tone of his voice. "It can't be!"

Puzzled, Jed glanced at Tap. "Can't be what?"

Tap kept staring at Charlie's face. "Your name's not Charlie! Not the one who busted up our camp last year?"

Jed kept glancing excitedly from Tap to Charlie. "Who's Charlie? What are you talking about, Tap? I wasn't with you last year."

"I'll tell you who Charlie is! He's Tom little brother and a one-man wrecking crew. That's who Charlie is! We've got to find a hole and bury him quick. We've done dabbed a rope on a cyclone, Jed. We'll be lucky to get back to camp without a broken leg or worse. He's jinxed, is what he is. Tom said he would shoot him himself if he ever came back to his camp again."

Realizing his dangerous position, Charlie spoke quickly. "He said that with one exception, Tap. He said that if I ever needed him real bad to call on him. Well, I'm needing to see him now. Besides… I've got money to pay him for what I want."

"The deuce you say!" Tap's eyes narrowed to hardly more than mere slits. "Just how much money have you got on you?"

"You never mind about how much money I've got. Are you gonna take me on to your camp or do I have to ride in alone?"

"Maybe we oughta take him in with us, Tap. Tom might get sore if it's something important. Especially if he's got money on him."

"Sore! I'll tell you what will happen if we take him into camp with us. Tom will shoot the both of us! You don't know this little firecracker, Jed. Why, he could start a forest fire in the middle of a lake. It gives me the jitters just being within a mile of him. I say we shoot him and drop his body in a wash close by."

Charlie's voice became sharper. "Go ahead, Tap. You pull the trigger. When Tom hears about it you'll be laying in a wash yourself. I told you that I got business with him."

Jed lifted his hand and rubbed the short stubble on his chin nervously. "Let's take him on in, Tap. I don't like shooting a kid, especially Tom's little brother."

"Alright, Jed but I'm warning you. It's going to be on your head. We'll live to regret this day. Instead of throwing a rope on him we should have emptied our rifles in him."

As Tap and Jed turned to get their horses, Charlie swung into the saddle with a wolfish grin on his face.

Without speaking anymore, Tap and Jed led the way in the direction of Tom's camp.

It was going on ten o'clock when the trio turned up the canyon. The night was white and still except for the weird shadows hanging on the canyon walls. It gave an eerie appearance, like a picture from some ancient, enchanted world.

They had covered almost a mile when Tap and Jed slowed their horses to a walk and a voice called from the shadows.

"Is that you Tap?"

"It's me. Jed and I picked up a visitor for Tom. He says it's mighty important."

They nudged their horses and continued up the canyon. A minute later they turned a bend and came into sight of the campfire.

"You stay behind, Charlie," said Tap as he turned in his saddle. "You can ride in after we've had a chance to talk to Tom. He may get a little upset."

Charlie dismounted as Tap and Jed rode on to the campfire. Leaving his horse ground hitched, he slipped through the shadows until he was within twenty-five feet of the fire. He hunkered down behind a huge rock and peered around it at the men sitting by the fire. There were three besides Tom. As he watched, Tap and Jed walked in.

Tom spoke without looking up. "Howdy, boys. Grab a cup of coffee and have a set." His voice was rough and hoarse. "Did you see who that was tailin' us?"

Tap picked up the coffee pot and began pouring himself a cup of coffee. He hesitated before speaking, glancing at Jed who reached for the pot. "Yeah, we found him, boss."

"I reckon you made buzzard meat out of him, uh? I don't like strangers foolin' around out here."

"We didn't shoot him. Had a chat with him first." Tap hunkered down beside the fire and kept giving Jed quick glances.

Jed became nervous and fixed his eyes on the fire, refusing to look anymore at Tap.

Suddenly Tom tensed, the cup in his hand freezing halfway to his mouth. After a few seconds he fastened his eyes on Tap and slowly set the cup on the ground. His eyes became brighter as he looked from Tap to Jed. "You boys got something to tell me? Like who this stranger was? Maybe if he was a friend or enemy?"

Tap took another slow sip of his coffee. "I can't rightly say which he was. In one way you could say he was a friend. In another way... an enemy." He took another swallow of his coffee and continued staring into the fire.

"Alright! Enough of the mystery talking!"

The other men around the fire tensed as they watched Tom's anger rising. They held their coffee cups still, afraid to move.

"Did this gent have a handle?"

Tap lifted his head and looked into Tom's eyes. "Yeah, boss. He answers to the name of Charlie."

Tom rose slowly to his feet, his eyes roving and his right hand dangling close to his gunbutt. "You wouldn't be meaning Charlie of Three Forks?"

Charlie saw Tap's perilous predicament and stuck his head out a few inches from the rock. He spoke lowly. "Tom."

His voice was answered by two sharp barks from Tom's gun. Quick as a flash he had drawn and shot, his bullets ricocheting from the rock where Charlie was hidden.

"Don't shoot, Tom! It's me... Charlie,

your brother." His voice was pleading.

"I know who you are," said Tom heatedly. "Come on out from behind that rock so I can plug you."

"Don't kill me, Tom. I've got to talk to you. I wouldn't have come but it's a matter of life or death. I've brought money with me too."

Tom stood staring at the rock with his gun leveled and ready to fire. Slowly the red anger began to subside and he holstered his gun, turning back to the fire.

Charlie peered out from behind the rock and saw Tom pouring himself another cup of coffee.

The men stared with wide eyes, afraid to speak for fear Tom might lose control of himself again.

Tom lifted the cup and took a swallow of the scalding liquid. His face winced slightly as the coffee burned its way down his throat. Without a backward glance in Charlie's direction he hunkered down and stared into the fire.

Charlie slipped silently to the campfire and hunkered down on his heels. After helping himself to a cup of coffee he sat in silence, staring at the small flames of the fire.

After a long minute Tom stole a quick glance at Charlie. His bright eyes softened as he looked again at the small hands wrapped around the coffee cup.

Another quick look and his eyes stayed on his little brother. He noted the shaggy red head and the smooth cheeks that were speckled with freckles. His thoughts returned to nine years ago when their Paw had been hung for horse stealing. Shortly afterwards their Ma had died. Since then he and Charlie had knocked about from here to yonder. Charlie didn't even know what it was like to have someone looking out for him. All he had ever had was a big brother and so far that had meant nothing for him. As he continued to stare at Charlie his face began to smooth out and the furrows left his brow.

"You know what I told you about ever coming to my camp again. It's no place for a kid."

Charlie spoke without looking at Tom. "I had to come. Just wasn't no way around it. You're the only one who can help me."

"What kind of trouble are you in? The law's not after you, are they?"

"No, it's not my trouble really. It's a friend of mine. We've got big trouble. We need your help."

Tom sipped slowly from his coffee cup. "This friend of yours. Who is he and what's the trouble?"

"It's not a he, Tom. It's a woman. A good, warm-hearted lady. Mighty pretty too. Her man got himself killed and she's needing help."

"A woman friend, uh?" Tom glanced at the men quickly to see their reaction to Charlie's words.

They were casually drinking their coffee, seemingly unconscious of the conversation going on.

"Now I'm wondering what this woman could possibly mean to you?"

"First, she's my friend. Secondly, she's my boss. I've got me a regular job now. I'm a cowhand."

Charlie's words broke the tension among the men and they grinned widely as they continued to listen.

"A cowhand you say. And a gun-toting one at that." Tom's voice became hard again. "Where'd you get that gun?"

"I borrowed it from my boss. I had to shoot a man the other night. He and some others attacked the ranch. They killed one of our hands and stole our cattle. My boss is feeling real low about now. She don't deserve to go under, Tom. We need your help." Charlie finally turned and looked into Tom's eyes. "I can't pay you much but I'll give you all I got. I've been saving it up for quite some time." He reached into his back pocket and pulled out the three dollars, then reached them to Tom. "It's all I have but it's yours if you will help me."

Tom reached out and took the money. After looking at it he held it in his open palm for all the men to see. "You see this, boys? Three whole dollars is what it is. Little Charlie wants to hire us. How about it?"

The men's faces brightened with pleasure.

"Just how long do we have to work for all that, boss?" asked Mike as he set his coffee cup down.

"Until the job's done," spoke Charlie quickly. "I don't figure it will take long with you men at work." He looked admiringly at Tom. "Heck, Tom's worth a half dozen men all by himself."

Charlie's words touched Tom deeper than the smiling men realized. They were words that had been spoken out of love and admiration.

"Just this once, Tom. I'll never bother you again unless you call for me."

Tom set his cup on the ground and jingled the coins in his hand. "What I want to know is… who this woman is that you're so fond of?"

Charlie swallowed hard, then took a deep breath before answering. "Bonnie Drake of the Rocking D."

Tom dropped the three dollars as he quickly jerked up his head and looked at Charlie. "The Rocking D?"

The men broke out in loud laughter. For three months they had been working along with Major Colter in stripping the Rocking D of their cattle. Sheriff Metters had been paid by Colter to keep his head turned and his gun holstered. Now here was Charlie wanting them to go to work for the ranch they had been plundering.

"You don't know what you're asking, Charlie. The boys and me… we can't go to work for the Rocking D. I can't explain why."

"You don't have to make any explanations. I've got eyes. I followed our cattle out here myself. She's a fine lady, Tom. You'd like her too."

Tom stood to his feet. "I'll tell you what. I'll think about it. I'll give you my answer in the morning."

At Tom's words the men's smiles vanished and they glanced at one another curiously. A slight smile touched the corners of Tap's lips as he rose to make his bed.

"Much obliged, Tom. I'll go get my horse." Charlie walked out of the camp as the other men started unrolling their beds.

Charlie opened his eyes to the still and silent morning. The sun was already up. He looked around and saw the camp was empty except for himself and Tom.

Tom was sitting with a cup of coffee gripped in his big hands and staring at him. When he spoke his words were hard and quick. "My men almost quit on me last night. I told them I wanted to help you out just this one time. No more! Just this once! I reckon you know what we'll have to do with all those Rocking D cattle we've got holed up?"

"They'll have to be returned but you won't regret it, Tom. I'll make it up to you someday."

Tom stood to his feet and poured the remaining coffee on the red coals of the fire. "You can ride on back to the ranch and tell Mrs. Drake everything's gonna work out okay for her. Don't speak my name or any of the men's names to her or anyone. You hear me, Charlie?"

"Sure, Tom, I hear you." He slipped to his feet and began rolling up his bed. After he had it rolled and tied he walked near Tom and reached out his hand. "Thanks, Tom. We'll shake on it."

Tom took the small hand and shook it. "This'll probably be the death of me but I reckon no man can expect to live forever. You skedaddle on back to the ranch now. The boys and me will start drifting in later."

Little Charlie

Chapter Four

It had been five days since leaving Tom's camp that Charlie rode into the ranch yard of the Rocking D. The ranch looked deserted and empty. Weber was no where in sight and Bonnie's mare was not in the corral.

He slid from the saddle and walked to the door. His knocking brought no response. As he headed for the barn he was troubled by disturbing thoughts. Something must have happened while he had been away.

Bonnie's mare was not in the barn. As he stepped back outside he lifted his face against the faint, cool breeze. He would have to ride into town. Someone must know of Bonnie's whereabouts.

Two hours later Charlie rode down the dusty street of Three Forks. It was mid-morning and the sun was heating up the day. He saw no sign of Weber's sorrel hitched in front of the saloon.

He started to turn his horse in at Maria's when he saw Bonnie's mare hitched in front of the bank. He gouged the mustang sharply and galloped toward it.

He had already left the saddle before the horse stopped. Leaving the reins trailing along the ground, he leaped to the boardwalk and rushed through the door.

Bonnie was nowhere in sight. There was a door which led into Mr. Brown's office and he walked slowly toward it. He was within five feet of the door when a voice called roughly from a few feet away.

"Hey, kid! Get away from that door!"

Charlie glanced in the direction of the voice and saw Major Colter's two lieutenants advancing upon him. Without answering he darted for the door and leaped inside.

The Major and Bonnie were sitting together and facing Mr. Brown. On his desk lay several papers and he was handing one to Bonnie.

"Just sign right there, Mrs. Drake and that should complete the transaction. I sure hate to see you lose your ranch but the Major is giving you a fair price for it."

Little Charlie

The big smile suddenly vanished from Colter's face as Charlie leaped to Bonnie's side. He whispered low in her ear as Mr. Brown and Colter looked on with both angry and shocked expressions on their faces. He stepped back, waiting for Bonnie's reply. "We better ride now. Time's wasting.

"Here now! What's the meaning of this?" Colter stood to his feet. "Charlie, you little scamp! You can't bust in on a meeting like this!" His voice was filled with anger as he glanced at the open door. "Stu! Shep! Where in the sam-hill are you?"

The two men stepped through the doorway. Their faces were red and they gave Charlie a murderous look.

Shep pointed a finger at Charlie. "That little coyote slipped by us, Major. We didn't think about him sitting in on you until he got close to the door."

"Get him out of here! Tie him up and throw him out in the street! He's almost spoiled our meeting."

Bonnie rose quickly and put her arm around Charlie's shoulder. "No need for that, Major. Charlie and I were leaving together." She looked at Mr. Brown. "I reckon you better hold those papers, Mr. Brown. Something's come up and I won't be signing them today."

Colter looked at his men, his face purple in rage as Bonnie and Charlie walked out of the office. "Two more minutes and we could've started pushing cattle on the Rocking D. Now we've got to wait again. All because of that... that brat of a Charlie." He strode from the room with his face dark with anger. With ever step he took he kept repeating the name to himself. "Charlie... Charlie." As the name fell from his lips his hand fondled his gunbutt.

Three days later from Charlie's return, Weber came pounding into the yard on a lathered horse and yelling loudly. "Mrs. Drake! Mrs. Drake!"

The door opened and Bonnie rushed outside with her rifle in her hand.

Weber leaped from his horse and ran to meet her. "I'll saddle your mare, Mrs. Drake. You've got to ride out and take a look at something." He looked at the gun in her hands. "You won't need that. Sorry I spooked you but I knew that you want to see this."

Bonnie set the rifle on the porch and waited as Weber saddled her horse.

The two raced from the yard toward the southern range.

Ten minutes later Bonnie saw them coming. In front of a large dust cloud came a slow-moving herd of cattle in their direction.

Weber grinned happily. "Little Charlie's leading them, boss. There's about a half dozen hands bringing them in. That's some of your rustled cattle. I'd say there's nigh onto a thousand head in that bunch. Charlie said there'd be more coming in later."

Bonnie's chin quivered slightly as she listened to Weber's words. Charlie had done it! He had performed a miracle. As her eyes misted over she spoke to Weber without turning her head. "I'd be pleased if you wouldn't mention anything about this or the men who are with the cattle."

"Don't you worry, boss. My mouth's a closed trap. It sure is a pretty sight though. I'm pleased for you."

"See that the cattle are brought in close. I don't think there will be need for a night guard though."

"Yes, ma'am. I'll go tell Charlie now."

As Weber spurred his horse in the direction of the cattle Bonnie turned back toward the ranch. She had gone only a short distance when she heard the rapid tatooing of horse's hooves drawing close behind her. She slowed her horse and turned.

A crooked grin played on Charlie's mouth as he slowed his mustang and joined Bonnie. "We did it, Bonnie! We're gonna save the ranch!" The freckles on his face were bright and beaming as his light blue eyes sparkled.

"It's more like you saved it, Charlie. If it hadn't been for you I wouldn't have a ranch any longer."

"Well, I'm glad we're friends. By the way, a certain fellow says he needs to talk to you. He said about ten o'clock tonight if that would be okay with you. He can't be seen around these cattle and neither can his men. That's the reason he wanted to come in after dark."

"You tell that certain fellow I'll be waiting and have the coffee hot."

Charlie grew silent and nervous.

Bonnie sensed that there was something else on his mind so she remained quiet and kept her eyes from him.

After a long minute had passed Charlie seemed to have gotten up his nerve. "I don't hardly know how to say this, Bonnie, but... that certain fellow...he means a lot to me. He may be kinda rough and all but he's got a heart. Sometimes I think he hates me but down deep inside he may have feelings for me like I do him. I'd like for you two to become friends. Like you and me."

"I see no reason why we shouldn't be, Charlie. I'll do my best. Okay?"

"Much obliged, Bonnie. Well, I better be getting back and tell him that ten o'clock is okay with you." He turned his horse and raced back toward the cattle.

Bonnie slipped on her light green gown and began drying her hair. She wondered about the late night visitor who would soon be coming. What would he be like and why was it so important to Charlie that they become friends? She smiled as she thought about Charlie and his mysterious recovery of her cattle.

She glanced at the clock and saw that it was almost ten when she heard the light tapping on the front door. She had no idea why she had suddenly become so nervous. Quickly she slid into her light blue calico dress and walked to the door. After taking a deep breath she opened the door.

The man who stood facing her was big. His faded, blue-checkered shirt was stretched tightly over his chest and shoulders that were heavy with muscle. His rough and unkempt appearance made him resemble a great lobo wolf.

Tom quickly jerked his hat off and a lock of brown, curly hair fell over his forehead.

As Bonnie looked into his light green eyes that were enhanced by small, yellow gleams it made her heart skip a beat.

"Reckon you must be Ms. Bonnie Drake. I'm Tom, the man who brought your cattle in."

"Yes, I'm Ms. Drake. Please come in, Mr..."

"Tom will do just fine, Ms. Drake." He stepped inside.

"Have a seat and I'll get you some coffee." Bonnie turned quickly and walked toward the kitchen.

Tom inhaled deeply of the fragrant air. The faint fragrance of Bonnie's perfume was pleasant. He took a seat and quickly finger-combed his hair.

As Bonnie stepped into the kitchen she brushed back a strand of hair that had fallen out of place. She breathed easier as she stepped from view of Tom. It had been a long time since a man had affected her this way. His eyes and smile were very becoming, even charming. Before pouring the coffee she took another deep breath to settle her shaken nerves.

Tom rose from his seat as she entered the room again with the coffee.

"Here you go." The cup trembled slightly in her shaking fingers.

"Much obliged, ma'am. I had a few things to tell you about the circumstances concerning your cattle. We've been hired by Charlie to work for you a spell."

"Hired by Charlie? My heavens, where did Charlie get enough money to hire a half dozen cowhands?"

"He's a wonder, ma'am. By the way… just in case something should happen to me, give this to him." Tom handed her a sealed envelope. "It's what he paid us to come and work for you. My men and I will have to work kind of undercover. We can't be seen on the range for awhile, especially by Major Colter. He will eventually have the sheriff out here after us but we'll try to get things set up right for you before he does."

Bonnie laid the envelope on the small center

table and turned to face Tom again as he sat back down. "Why should he do that?" she asked with a puzzled expression on her face.

"He wants this ranch, ma'am, and he intends to have it. Those were his men who attacked your ranch the other night."

A grim expression spread across her face as she recalled her previous conversations with Colter and his ceaseless efforts to buy her out.

Tom swallowed the last of his coffee and stood to his feet. "I guess I better be going now."

Bonnie stood up quickly. "Do you have to leave so soon? There's more coffee."

He fondled his hat nervously as he looked into her eyes.

She watched the small beads of sweat appear on his brow and felt suddenly relieved inside. She could tell he liked her and the thought made her even more nervous. "When will I be seeing you again?"

"Soon. My men and I will be around but we'll be keeping out of sight." He turned and stepped to the door and opened it. "Goodnight, ma'am."

"Goodnight." As the door closed Bonnie stood for a long moment staring at it.

Tom gripped the reins tightly in his hand and climbed into the saddle. As he turned his horse to the open range he sighed deeply, thinking about the situation at hand. It would be 'tuck and run' for a spell now but it seemed to have always been that way for him.

Little Charlie

Chapter Five

Colter sat in the Silver Spur saloon seething in anger as he faced Sheriff Metters. "What I want to know is where all those cattle are coming from? She must have a thousand head back on her southern range. And another thing... what's Tom doing?"

"No one has seen him, Major. Dave's not checked in with me for almost two weeks. I can't figure out what's happened to him."

"Get Deputy Forbes out on the trail toward Tom's camp and see if he can locate anyone. I want to know what's going on."

Metters fidgeted nervously in his seat as he watched the rising passion in Colter's face. "I'll send him out first thing in the morning but no one knows where Tom's camp is located. He's not the trusting kind."

"I've got a hunch that brat of a Charlie is mixed up some way or another in this. He spoiled everything in the bank. I'd give a hundred dollars to know what he whispered to Ms. Drake that day."

"The next time he's in town I'll latch on to him. He and Weber are the only ones I spotted out on the range yesterday. There's something fishy going on. We'll have to keep our eyes open."

A slight, foxy smile appeared on Colter's face. "I'm planning on doing a little snooping and night riding myself. I intend to get to the bottom of this. I want that ranch and I aim to have it… regardless of what it takes."

Colter finished his drink and stood to his feet. He motioned for his two men at the bar to follow and strode from the saloon.

The three men sat in silence on the low ridge top and watched as the light went out in the bunkhouse below. It was ten o'clock and the moon was rising steadily overhead brightening up the night.

Colter stood to his feet. "Weber's gone to bed, boys. The house looks to be empty except for Ms. Drake but I've got a hunch someone is in there with her. Stu, you stay with the horses while Shep and I have a look."

The two men slipped silently off the hill. Their roving eyes detected no movement around the yard. The place was silent and nothing broke the stillness.

Shep paused in the shadows of the large cottonwood as Colter advanced to the window.

As Colter drew near the lighted window he heard low voices inside. A smile of triumph touched his lips as he lifted his head to peer inside.

He saw Bonnie sitting at the table and facing her was Charlie. No one else was in sight. Their smiling faces enraged him. He touched the butt of his gun, tempted to draw it and shoot the little rascal through the window. He had become a thorn in his side every since he had found Ms. Drake by the creek, shot and unconscious. Ever since then it seemed that things had been looking up for her. He gritted his teeth as the black thoughts washed across his mind. He'd take care of the little red-headed meddler. With him out of the way Ms. Drake would soon be out of business.

After giving the pair another murderous look he motioned for Shep to follow and slipped back to the hilltop.

As they rode away Colter reached a decision. "Tomorrow night, boys. Little Charlie will be removed tomorrow night."

It was nearing midnight as the three men walked their horses quietly into the ranch yard of the Rocking D. There were no lights showing and the ranch lay silent, sleeping under the silvery moon.

A lone coyote sent his shrill, lonesome call upward, then waited for its echo.

The intruders pushed open the bunkhouse door and stepped quietly inside. After a long moment their ears picked up the slow, even breathing of the two sleepers who presented no more than dark forms in the shadowed room.

Charlie lay on his back with his mouth partly open and one arm hanging off the side of the bed. Suddenly his eyes opened wide as a big, rough hand closed over his mouth. A low, throaty grunt was all he could manage to voice as he felt other hands binding his ankles with a piece of rawhide. After his feet were secured the men bound his wrists together.

He fought against his abductors by kicking

out with his bound feet. It was no use. His mouth felt like it had been placed in a vise. He was jerked from the bed and quickly carried outside.

Weber stirred and then opened his eyes. As he did he felt the hard impact of the gun barrel crash against the side of his head. He started to rise but sank helplessly down again. He felt the warm, slow trickle of blood running down the side of his face, then darkness washed over his eyes.

The man stood over Weber for a long moment, then turned and walked outside.

The three men wore grim, determined faces. Their orders had been clear and concise. 'Get Charlie! If not, don't ever show your faces on the Bar C again. Ever!'

They walked their horses from the yard silently.

Charlie stared into the face of the man who held him tightly in his arms. His body was aching from the rough rocking of the racing horse as the miles passed swiftly behind him. The hand had been taken from his mouth.

He saw the great mesa stretching upward against the skyline in the near distance and spoke for the first time. "Where are you men taking me?"

The voice of the man was rough. "You'll find out when we get there, kid."

"I ain't bothered anyone. What do you aim to do with me?" There was a slight trace of fear in Charlie's voice.

"We're taking you on a vacation, boy. It seems you need to get away and rest up for a spell. You've been working too hard lately. Your meddling has started getting on people's nerves."

The men slowed their horses as they drew near the base of the mesa and dismounted. The scattering of huge boulders permitted enough cover to conceal a hundred men. They led their horses slowly through the maze of rocks for a hundred yards and came in sight of the giant, red wall that rose upward for several hundred feet.

At the base of the wall was a large, hollowed out place which looked like a giant, battering ram had smashed a great hole in it. The cavern was twenty feet wide and reached thirty feet to the rear. A small trickle of water flowed from a crack in the inside wall and filled a shallow basin, then disappeared again through another crack. It was a perfect hideaway.

"Lloyd, while we unsaddle the horses, I

reckon you may as well build a fire and get some beans and bacon on," said Chuck as he lowered Charlie to the ground. "It won't be long until first light and we'll have to keep a guard posted day and night. After we eat we'll grab a couple of hours shuteye and then make the place comfortable. We may be here for a spell."

The one called Jasper fixed hard eyes on Charlie. His voice was harsh when he spoke. "The Major's already warned us about you, boy. We're going to start off by leaving your hands and feet tied. You behave yourself and we might decide to untie you later. If you start acting up we may just go ahead and shoot you. I kinda favor that idea myself. I don't particular like playing nursemaid to a kid anyhow."

Charlie looked into the narrow, mean eyes of Jasper and decided he was the meanest of the three. Chuck seemed to be the leader of the three and in command. He was the serious one and all business. Lloyd would be the one he would have to work on. The way he watched and listened to the other two made one wonder if he didn't have a younger brother or sister somewhere that he had left behind.

The men ate a hurried meal and spread their

ground sheets.

Charlie still sat with his back against the wall. The reflection of the dimming fire cast weird shadows around the cave-like enclosure. He gave Chuck a quick glance. "You got the makings for another bed, Chuck?"

"No, kid, I surely don't. You'll just have to curl up there on the ground." He stretched his tired body on the bed. "I wouldn't think you'd need to worry about getting cold though. The last time I spent the night here there were enough scorpions and spiders to keep a man warm."

His words brought a loud guffaw from Jasper who added quickly. "That's right, boy, not to mention that rattler we saw. He had enough rattles on him to make a good-sized bracelet. If I were you I wouldn't sleep to sound. You may never wake up."

It was two hours past first light as Bonnie walked across the yard to the bunkhouse. She had neither seen nor heard Charlie and Weber all morning. She wondered what was keeping them from breakfast.

As she stepped inside the door and saw

Weber stretched on his bunk with a bloody face she gasped loudly and ran to his side. Her eyes fell on the large lump on the side of his head. Glancing quickly at Charlie's bed she saw that it was empty.

A wave of panic swept over her. After examining Weber more closely she realized he was not simply unconscious. He was dead.

She left the bunkhouse in a stumbling run for the corral, her mind a mad confusion of troubled thoughts. She must report the murder to the sheriff and the apparent kidnapping of Charlie. After that she intended to try and find Tom. She threw the saddle on the mare quickly and raced in the direction of Three Forks.

An hour later as Bonnie drew near Running Water Creek a rider dropped off the low ridge and headed in her direction. It was Tom.

Tom halted his horse and waited on Bonnie. As he waited he reached into his pocket for the makings and rolled himself a cigarette. He had been thinking of her quite a bit and was taken in by her beauty. He liked her pleasant voice, her charming smile, and the graceful movements with which she carried herself. As she pulled her horse to a halt he dubbed his cigarette on the saddle horn. "Morning, Ms. Drake. Looks like you're in a big hurry."

"Tom, I'm glad you're here. Weber was killed during the night and Charlie's missing. I believe he's been kidnapped. I was on my way to report it to the sheriff." Her eyes became filled with tears. "What are we gonna do about Charlie?"

"Well, ma'am, if he was kidnapped and not killed I'd say someone is in big trouble. Things have a way of happening around him. Strange things."

"Oh, nonsense! Every since I've been around Charlie I've had good luck and things have been going better for me."

"I reckon you're the first then. Take my word for it... if someone has kidnapped him that man or men won't come back all in one piece. That is, if they come back at all."

"I'm afraid for him, Tom. These men meant business. They killed Weber and they'll kill Charlie too. It would pretty nigh be the death of me if anything happened to him. Would you try and find him? I've become rather fond of him."

"Maybe I could ride out and take a look, Ms. Drake. I was fixing to take the boys and go get the rest of your cattle but I guess it can wait for another day or two. You ride on to town. I'll ride back to the ranch and see if I can pick up any tracks."

"Thanks, Tom. I know that Charlie will be grateful too." She headed the mare on to Three Forks.

Little Charlie

Chapter Six

Major Colter stood silently in the door of the Silver Spur and watched Bonnie race down the street. He smiled as he saw her leap from her saddle in front of the sheriff's office. As he watched her rush inside he turned back and headed for his table to join Shep and Stu.

Shep finished his drink and looked into the triumphant face of Colter. "I guess that was Ms. Drake riding in."

"It was. With that little coyote of a Charlie out of the way I'll have her ranch yet. You boys get some of the men ready to ride when we get back to the ranch. This time when those Rocking D cattle disappear they won't mysteriously show up again. Tell the boys to trail them on in to Amarillo and sell them." He turned and walked back to the door to see Bonnie and Metters' loping out of town. After motioning for Shep and Stu to follow, he walked outside.

While Jasper was out rustling a few tufts of the short, coarse grass for the horses a mile from the camp and Chuck was on the look-out above the camp, Charlie began working on Lloyd. "My hands are numb, Lloyd. Can't you untie them for a little while?"

"I don't know about that, Charlie. Chuck's idea was to leave you tied up."

"I can't very well go any place with my legs hobbled. Besides, I could help you with supper if my hands were free."

"I reckon I could let you peel a few potatoes. I'll have to tie you back up though before the boys come in. That Jasper... he's a mean sort and easy riled. You don't want to make him mad, Charlie. He'd shoot you quick." He reached down and untied Charlie's hands. "You sit right there and I'll bring the spuds to you."

Charlie rubbed his wrists and hands to get the circulation going again. His searching eyes began looking for a possible weapon or other means of escape. He had to get away and back to the ranch. There was no telling what Colter was up to.

He looked up innocently as Lloyd brought the pan of potatoes and set them beside him. He tried to sound frightened as he spoke. "Do you reckon Chuck's gonna turn me loose when this is over?"

"I don't know. We'll have to wait and see. Jasper will be agin it though. Like I said before, he's a mean one. Killing a kid wouldn't bother him none a'tall."

The afternoon passed swiftly and when supper was almost ready Lloyd took the piece of rawhide and bound Charlie's wrists again. There was a slight trace of regret in his eyes as he bound the small hands together. "Sorry, Charlie. Jasper will be coming in with the horses anytime now."

Lloyd stood to his feet, then paused, listening. They heard the sharp ring of shod horses coming through the rocks. A minute later Jasper appeared, leading the horses.

After letting the horses drink from the shallow basin Jasper led them to the rear of the enclosure and tied them. His dark eyes fastened on Charlie as he turned and spoke to Lloyd. "That supper shor' smells good. I'm half starved. The kid ain't give you no trouble today, has he?"

"None a'tall, Jasper." He glanced quickly at Charlie. "He's been quiet as a mouse at a Sunday meeting."

"Too bad." He grinned wolfishly at Charlie as he stepped closer. "I was hoping I'd have reason to plug him. Kids always did get on my nerves. I never did like 'em."

Lloyd gave Charlie another fleeting look as he stepped to the front of the cavern. "I'll go on up and relieve Chuck so he can come to supper." He disappeared among the rocks outside.

A minute later Chuck walked in with his rifle tucked under the hollow of his arm. He propped it against the wall and began filling his plate as he spoke to Jasper. "Find enough feed for the horses?"

"Yeah, enough I reckon. After another couple of days I'll have to find another spot though."

Chuck sat down and leaned against the wall. He looked at Charlie as he lifted a spoonful of potatoes to his mouth. "You et yet, Charlie?"

"No. Lloyd said I'd have to wait for you to untie my hands."

"I reckon we could trust you that long. I'm warning you though… you give us any trouble and we'll leave you up in the rocks for the buzzards." He rose and untied his hands.

Jasper smiled. This was very much to his liking. The only way to handle kids was with a big stick and a ready gun.

The group of horsemen rode from the yard of the Bar C. There were seven in all and all wore dark clothes and rode dark horses.

Duke Clemmons led the cavalcade whose mission was directed toward the Rocking D. With Weber dead and Charlie out of the way the ranch would be empty except for Ms. Drake.

Darkness had already settled in as the riders circled the resting herd. Within minutes the cattle were on their feet and beginning to move toward the eastern range of the Bar C and in the direction of Amarillo.

Inside the ranch house Bonnie lay with her eyes open and her thoughts a jumbled mass of mixed emotions.

She frowned at the thoughts of Colter

playing her for a light-headed fool. His seemingly concern for her welfare by giving her more than a fair price for her ranch angered her. All the time he had been behind the rustling of her cattle and probably had the sheriff involved in the scheme. She recalled how Metters could never seem to find out anything about the rustlers. Had it not been for Charlie she would already have lost the ranch she had worked so hard for.

Her thoughts returned to Tom; the big, rough outlaw and rustler who was even now helping her. She still had been unable to spot any of his men on the range.

With Weber and Charlie gone she felt isolated, lonely, and quite forsaken.

She sighed lowly and pulled the sheet tighter around her neck as she watched the curtains move slightly under the touch of the rippling breeze. She seemed to detect a faint scent of dust in the air. As her eyes grew heavier and slowly closed a steer bawled off in the distance. Then another one. Like a beckoning call for their master they moved within hearing of the ranch but Bonnie never heard them. She had fallen asleep.

It was early morning and Jasper had taken the horses out again. Chuck was on the lookout rock and Lloyd was busy scouring the pans at the small pool.

After much coaxing Charlie had finally managed to persuade Lloyd to untie both his hands and feet. As he continued to occupy Lloyd with his many questions, his mind was busy trying to conceive a plan of escape. Suddenly his eyes fell on the frying pan. It was a weapon; a weapon that had proved efficient on more than one occasion.

As he picked up the knife he had used in peeling the potatoes Lloyd lifted his eyes.

"Now what might you be thinking about with that knife in your hand, Charlie? You wouldn't be thinking of hiding it inside ole Lloyd's gizzard, would you?"

"Ah, I couldn't do nothing like that, Lloyd. What do you take me for?"

"A boy that would like to hightail it back to the Rocking D is what I take you for. I'd say that whatever you had to do to get there wouldn't bother you none a'tall. You seem to be mighty fond of that lady boss of yours."

"She's a fine lady. You'd like her too if you got to know her."

"Well, it ain't likely ole Lloyd will ever get

to know her any better than he does right now. Women folks never gave me more than a passing glance. Reckon I don't have what catches their eye. Now about that knife there… I guess you better hand it over here before you get any fancy ideas." He reached out his hand for the knife.

"Sure, Lloyd." He reached out his hand and took a step toward him. Suddenly his foot rolled on a small stone and threw him off balance. As his arms swung out the knife spun out of his hand and fell into the basin of water. His right hand landed just behind Lloyd's back and next to the frying pan. Quickly his fingers wrapped around the handle.

"Now doggone it, Charlie! Look what you've done!" Lloyd rolled up his sleeve to the elbow and reached into the water to retrieve the knife. With his head lowered and his eyes glued on the knife he never saw the movement of Charlie as he brought the pan down hard on his head. He slumped sideways to the ground and lay still.

Chuck strained his eyes against the glare of

the sun and watched the rising dust cloud drawing nearer. It was moving in the general direction of the mesa but he knew it would begin turning south before it got to within a mile of where he sat. It was the rustled herd of the Rocking D. The Major had told them it would be heading this way on its trek to Amarillo.

His rifle lay propped in the shadow of the rock beside him. The rocks were already hot under the burning sun and soon he would have to change positions.

He sat in silence and watched the moving dust cloud. Suddenly his thoughts were stilled by the cocking of a pistol and a rough voice behind him.

"Just keep your hands where I can see them, mister. No use turning around."

As the voice spoke, Chuck's fingers moved across the handle of the small hunting knife he carried in the top of his boot. It was an idea he had adopted from a Mexican in San Antonio. It had a heavy four-inch blade that was razor sharp on both sides. A quick flick of the wrist was all that was needed to bury it to the hilt inside a man's body.

The big man behind Chuck silently slid his gun back into its holster and drew the bone-handled knife from the sheath he carried on his belt. He stepped closer to Chuck. He knew about those boot knives some men carried. He had been south of the border himself. He saw the slight movement of Chuck's right arm and knew what was coming.

Chuck turned swiftly, the boot knife gripped for throwing. He realized he was too late as the bowie was hurled from Tom's palm. It lodged in his belly, buried to the hilt.

As the big knife struck him in the midsection, Chuck's right hand flew upward and the small boot knife slid from his fingers. It went high into the air.

The knife soared like a small silver bird and twinkled in the bright sunlight. End over end it sailed upward, then, pausing for a second it speeded back down toward the rocks. The handle landed hard as it struck a large boulder and bounced high into the air again. It fell lower among the rocks and each time it landed it bounced again. Finally it fell to the ground a few yards from the entrance of the cavern.

Chapter Seven

Jasper's brow was covered with sweat as he sat in the shadow of the rock and watched the horses cropping short grass. The beginning of a frown spread across his face as he tried to figure out what was gnawing on his mind.

He had seen something over supper last night. Something had been out of place. His eyes had swept across something that had raised a doubt, a question in his mind. It had been a fleeting thing and forgotten until this morning.

Inch by inch his mind searched every foot of the camp as he tried to recall every word of conversation that had been spoken. Suddenly his eyes opened wider. Charlie! That was it! He remembered now.

He had been watching Chuck when he untied Charlie's hands to eat supper. The marks made by the rawhide bindings were hardly visible. Then there was the way he had used his hands immediately after being untied. They should have been stiff, sore, and harder to move. Lloyd must have been untying his hands during the day and tying them back again before he and Chuck returned to camp. That had to be it! Somehow or other that little red-headed rooster had gotten through to Lloyd.

He jumped to his feet and quickly and retrieved the ropes of the horses and turned toward camp.

An hour later Jasper tied the horses below the camp and moved silently in. He heard no sound of voices from either Lloyd or Charlie. Then his eye caught the bright reflection of an object in front of the entrance. 'Chuck's boot knife,' he whispered to himself. 'He must've dropped it this morning'.

Suddenly he paused at the sound of a low, scraping noise inside. The sound of something being dragged across the ground. He drew his gun and stepped from around the last rock from the side of the entrance.

As he peered inside he saw Lloyd

propped against the wall, tied and gagged. Charlie was busy tying his feet.

Lloyd's eyes were hard and bright with anger. The veins in his neck and forehead swelled and turned darker as he tried to speak through the gag.

"Sorry, Lloyd," spoke Charlie in a low voice. "I hate to leave you like this but I've got other business to attend to. You understand what I mean, don't you?"

"Ummm---uppphhhh!"

"Don't try to talk. It's bad on your heart right now," continued Charlie. "Chuck and Jasper will be here in a few hours and they'll let you loose. Sure wish I could get my hands on one of those horses. I prefer riding to walking."

"I wouldn't be worrying about either one, kid."

Charlie spun around quickly at Jasper's voice behind him.

"When I get through with you, you ain't going to be doing either one."

Charlie's face and eyes filled with fear as he stared at Jasper. He could see the hate and yet, there was a twinkle of pleasure in his eyes. The dark muzzle of the gun was aimed at his head and steady as a rock.

Little Charlie

"Got ole Lloyd all trussed up, uh? I had me a feeling you were up to no good. Yessir, I was sitting there thinking this morning and said to myself, 'Jasper, ole son, you better go check on Lloyd. He may be in trouble'. Looks like my hunch paid off."

Jasper stepped closer, grinning wickedly. "Get up, you little coyote! I'm going to take you up in the rocks where the buzzards won't have any trouble finding your measly carcass. Come suppertime our playing nursemaid to you will be over."

"I reckon you won't have to wait until supper, mister." The voice behind Jasper was rough. "Maybe all your nursemaid playing days are over."

Jasper's gun remained trained on Charlie. "Better drop that gun you're holding on me, whoever you are. I can't miss the kid even if you shoot me in the back."

"Go ahead, Tom, and shoot him!" Charlie stood to his feet. "He was planning on killing me anyway."

"Shut up!" Jasper's gun lifted slightly as Charlie stood up. "Even if he gets me there's still Chuck. You ain't ever going back to the Rocking D."

"No use in looking for Chuck if that was

his name," said Tom. "The last thing I saw when I left the rocks above were dark shadows swinging lower out of the sky."

"Lloyd!" As Charlie yelled he dove for the ground.

The sudden exclamation from Charlie slowed Jasper's reflex for a split second.

It was what Charlie had hoped for. The bullet intended for his heart splattered rock splinters behind the spot where he had been standing.

The first bullet from Tom's gun hit Jasper in the right shoulder, spinning him around. The second drilled a hole through his chest on the left side.

Jasper fell hard upon the rocky and sandy ground. He lifted his eyes and glared at Tom. "You were supposed to be working for the Major. He'll hang you for this."

"He'll be lucky if he's not hanged himself. Murdering women and kids is frowned upon in Texas. His greed is going to be the knife that cuts his own throat." As he spoke he shucked the empties from his gun and reloaded it.

Small spots of blood appeared at the corners of Jasper's mouth. His eyes rolled back and his head slumped sideways on the ground. His outstretched leg gave one slight, shuddering jerk and then he lay still.

"Not a bad move you made there, boy." Tom smiled at Charlie as he stood to his feet.

Charlie's face widened in a big grin and his freckles beamed brighter. In all of his thirteen years he had never had Tom to smile at him. He turned his head quickly so the small drops that were forming in his eyes could not be seen. After dusting himself off, he reached down and picked up Jasper's gun. "I reckon we oughta be riding. Bonnie will think we ain't ever coming back." He blinked his eyes to clear them before turning around.

"Bonnie will have to wait. We've got some cattle to take back with us. The Major's men picked them up at the ranch and are driving them to Amarillo. Tap and the boys are following them."

Charlie motioned toward Lloyd. "What about Lloyd here? What are we gonna do with him?"

"That's a good question. If we turn him loose he will head straight for the Major. Right now Colter doesn't know that I'm working for the Rocking D. I guess we could shoot him. He deserves it."

"He's the only one that treated me half right, Tom. He's not so bad." He walked over and removed the gag from Lloyd's mouth. "What's your plans? Allowing we turn you loose, that is."

"I'll be looking for another job when the Major finds out we let you escape. He may just shoot me himself. My life won't be worth much on this range any more."

"I guess Ms. Drake might take you on. With Weber gone, she needs a man on the ranch. You could stay close to the house until this trouble with Colter is settled. I reckon Chuck and Jasper evened things up for Crowley and Weber. Of course you might decide to doublecross Ms. Drake after you've had time to think things over." Tom paused, staring hard at him. "I'd have to kill you then."

Lloyd gave Charlie a quick look and grinned. "I don't know that working alongside of Charlie would be so bad. Might take you up on that job."

"Cut him loose, Charlie. You two skedaddle on back to the Rocking D. I'll join Tap and bring Ms. Drake's cattle back. Make sure no one sees you returning. If anyone should enquire, I've been no where around here. You understand? Colter will find out soon enough but let him keep guessing as long as time allows. Jasper left the horses in the rocks below." He walked quickly outside, leaving Charlie and Lloyd staring after him.

Chapter Eight

Bonnie sat on the porch looking out across the plains. The stars were out and the night was bright. She sipped slowly from her coffee, liking the cool, gentle breeze that caressed her brow.

There was activity on the range as horsemen moved across the great expanse in the distance but they were both unseen and unheard by Bonnie. The ranch lay empty, void of sound except for an occasional stamping of a horse in the corral.

Suddenly she lifted her head and listened intently. In the near distance came the sound of pounding hooves. They were hardly more than a faint tatoo but as she listened they drew nearer.

She finished the last of her coffee and set the cup beside her chair. The horses were drawing closer. She rose to her feet and stepped to the partly open door and retrieved the rifle that was propped beside it. After sitting back down with the rifle across her knees she continued to listen and wait.

The riders were a hundred yards away when she saw them. They presented no more than dark forms moving rapidly toward the house. As they drew closer she saw there were two of them. One was small and the other bigger. They were at the edge of the yard when she made out who the smaller one was. It was Charlie accompanied by a stranger.

Charlie saw Bonnie rise from her chair and he yelled. "Bonnie!" He was already out of the saddle when the horse slid to a halt. He rushed to the porch. "Are you okay?"

Bonnie smiled as she quickly laid the rifle in the chair and turned to face him. "I'm fine, Charlie. How about you? I've been worried sick about you."

"Never felt better in my whole life. Tom came for me just in time. Said to tell you he would be coming in later with your rustled cattle. He and his men are tailing them. It was that dadjim Major and his men." Suddenly he paused and glanced at Lloyd who was standing behind him. "Doggone, I'm sorry, Bonnie. Excuse my manners. This here is Lloyd. He used to be one of the Major's men but he's had a change of mind. Tom said that you might give him a job."

"Hello, Lloyd." Bonnie reached out her hand. "Yes, I think I can manage that." She turned back to Charlie. "Sit down here and tell me what on earth happened to you and where you've been."

Charlie gave her a brief recap on the events that had transpired the past few days. "Tom said for Lloyd to hang around the ranch and keep outa sight until this trouble with the Major is over. Reckon I'll have to do the same. He'll be in a rage when he finds out that I escaped."

The trio sat on the porch and talked away the night before they finally stood to their feet.

"I'm going to get some shuteye, Bonnie. I'm about tuckered out." He stretched his small frame and yawned.

Bonnie ran her hand through his hair and smiled tenderly at him. "I'll have breakfast waiting for you and Lloyd when you get up. Good-night, Charlie."

"Good-night, Bonnie."

Lloyd tipped his hat. "Night, Ms. Drake." He followed Charlie to the corral to unsaddle their horses.

Charlie glanced back at the porch to make sure Bonnie had gone inside. "I told you that you'd like her. You do, don't you, Lloyd?"

"She seems to be a fine lady, Charlie. This just might turn out to be a permanent roost for me."

After turning their horses into the corral they headed for the bunkhouse.

It was mid-morning as the stranger rode down the main street of Three Forks and pulled in at the Silver Spur saloon. He was a tall man, broad shouldered and narrow at the hips. As his light green eyes took in the town a yellow gleam rose up in them. He took his black, flat-brimmed hat from his sweaty head and blew a shallow layer of dust from it.

Sheriff Metters stood at the window and stared at the stranger. A slight frown creased his brow as he watched him slip the thong off the hammer of his gun. Even at this distance he could see the handles of the forty-five were well worn and polished from much use.

The stranger gave another brief, appraising glance over the town and, settling his hat on his head, stepped inside the saloon.

There were three Bar C hands standing at the bar as the stranger walked up and ordered himself a drink. The room was otherwise empty except for two other men who sat at a table in deep conversation and speaking in low tones.

Con Silvers poured the drink and gave the stranger a quick look.

"Looking for a riding job," spoke the stranger in a low, drawling voice. "Any ranches around here hiring?"

"Only two ranches close by. The Bar C and the Rocking D. Can't say whether or not they're hiring at the time. You might ride out and talk to Major Colter at the Bar C." He gave the bar another swipe with his rag and glanced at the three Bar C hands who had ceased talking.

The apparent leader of the three turned and looked at the stranger. "The Major ain't hiring and the Rocking D would be a plumb bad prospect, stranger. If I was you I'd just keep riding."

"I reckon you must be the ramrod of the

Bar C, uh?" He fastened his light, piercing eyes on the speaker as he swallowed a gulp of the burning liquid.

"No, just a friendly tip. You can take it or leave it."

He swallowed the last of his drink and set the glass down. "Much obliged for the tip and that's the way I'll take it; friendly. By the way, who's the owner of this Rocking D?"

"Her name's Bonnie Drake," came the voice of Metters as he stepped through the batwings and approached the bar. "Widow woman. Her husband was killed a few weeks ago in a gunfight in Amarillo. If I were you, stranger, I'd take Mort's advice and keep riding. Strangers ain't too welcome on the Bar C and Rocking D. We've been having some rustling trouble."

The stranger grinned faintly as he looked into Metters eyes. "Sounds like a plumb unfriendly country, sheriff." He threw two bits on the bar without taking his eyes from Metters. "Obliged for the advice." He walked from the saloon.

Metters and the three Bar C hands stepped quickly to the door and watched the stranger mount his horse. He took the south trail out of town. The trail leading to the Rocking D.

Two hours later the stranger pulled his horse up in front of the porch of the Rocking D. His roving eyes had taken in the range while riding in. He had seen no cattle, no cowhands, and there were but a half dozen horses in the corral. The buildings were in good shape but so far he had seen no one.

As he dismounted the door opened and Bonnie stood in the doorway with her rifle grasped tightly in her hands.

He tipped his hat as he spoke. "Howdy, ma'am. Looking for a riding job but judging from the lack of cattle on the range I'd say I'm out of luck."

"Maybe, maybe not. I'm Bonnie Drake, owner of the Rocking D. There will be cattle on the range in a day or two. Some got misplaced the other night but they'll be back shortly."

"My name's Riley. I asked in town if any ranches were hiring but the sheriff seemed to discourage any strangers from coming in. I reckon he had his reasons for it."

"I'm not surprised, Mr. Riley. The sheriff appears to have some strange ways and opinions. I might give you a job if you're interested. I may as well tell you beforehand though, it could be dangerous working for me. I had a man killed in the bunkhouse the other night and a young boy kidnapped. The boy's been rescued. The sheriff didn't show much consideration for the death of my hand."

"Well, I've confronted trouble before, Ms. Drake. It won't be anything new. How many hands have you got left?"

"Just the young boy, Charlie, and a new hand name Lloyd. You can find you a bed in the bunkhouse with them. They're out on the range but they should be coming in soon."

"Much obliged, ma'am. I'll be looking after my horse then." He turned and led his horse to the watering trough near the corral.

Bonnie stood gazing at the stranger for a long moment, then turned and closed the door.

Riley was rubbing down his horse and giving him the attention that he rightly deserved when Charlie and Lloyd rode in. He watched as they stripped their horses and turned them into the corral.

Charlie and Lloyd started for the house, then suddenly changed direction and walked over to join Riley.

A faint smile touched Riley's lips as he looked at Charlie and Lloyd. "Howdy, men. Name's Riley. Ms. Drake gave me a job. You must be Charlie and Lloyd."

Charlie studied Riley's face for a long moment before answering. "Reckon so, Mr. Riley. You're new around these parts, uh?"

"You got that right, Charlie. From down around Austin. Ever been down that way?"

"No. I ain't never been anywhere except on this range. I'm surely not a long-riding man."

Riley's grin grew wider. He liked this small, red-headed fellow and it showed in his eyes. "Well, boys, I think I'm gonna like working here with you all."

"We best get washed up then. Supper'll be ready in a little bit and I surely want to be ready. This is the first job I've ever had where I've been fed regular."

Tom and his men waited until the Bar C riders were preparing for bed. When they had spread their ground sheets and sat down over their last cup of coffee he stepped from the shadows.

Two of the rustlers were with the herd but

Kelly and Jim had been dispatched to take care of them.

Tom walked silently into the firelight and faced Duke Clemmons who sat with a cup of coffee in his hands. His voice was drawling and pleasant as he spoke. "Howdy, Duke. Working pretty far off your range, ain't you?"

"Tom!" Duke's surprise showed in his eyes and voice. "The Major's been looking all over for you. Where you been hiding out?"

"Here and yonder. Mostly yonder. I rode in to pick up some cattle. We had some to stray off a few nights ago."

Suddenly Clemmons grew tense. He slowly set his cup on the ground and stood to his feet. His eyes searched Tom's face for the meaning of his words.

One of the men sitting near Duke began easing his hand slowly toward his gun.

Tom caught the movement and spoke without looking at him. "I wouldn't do that, mister. This is between Duke and me."

"You must be loco, Tom! There's five men in this camp and two more riding herd."

"You had two with the cattle. They've been replaced by my men. My advice to all of you would be to slip your guns out of their holsters real carefully. Maybe I should warn you that there's guns trained on the lot of you right now."

The silent rage rose in Duke's eyes and his voice became sharp. "I think you're bluffing. I don't know what your game is but I'm taking these cattle on to Amarillo. Major's orders."

"Sorry to hear you say that, Duke."

The men around the fire saw the three rifle barrels appear behind where Duke stood. One of them started to warn Duke but too late.

As Tom finished speaking Duke's hand flashed for his gun. It was out of the holster and moving upward to a firing position when Tom's first bullet tore through his shirt pocket, taking the red button with it. The second bullet followed on its heels, striking one inch to the left of the first. Either one would have killed him.

His mouth flew open and his eyes widened as he took two steps backward before falling. He was dead before he hit the ground.

Tom looked over the rest of the men as he shucked the empties from his gun and reloaded it. "Any of you other boys got any objections to who's in control of those cattle?"

The men simply stared at him without speaking.

"Well, you've got two choices. You can ride

now and leave your guns behind or you can walk home. If you decide to ride I wouldn't want to be seeing you no time soon. What's it gonna be?"

"I'm for riding," spoke one of the men as he stood to his feet. "Heck, there's no way of winning against a stacked deck." He stepped closer to Tom. "If you have company on the range before you get back I won't be in the crowd."

"I'll remember that," said Tom. "What's your name?"

"Dorsky. Pete Dorsky." He unbuckled his gun and let it fall to the ground. He noted the disapproval written on the other men's faces but he was playing a hunch. It was a hunch that seemed to be whispering a bad omen for Major Colter of the Bar C.

Chapter Nine

It had been two days since the Major's men had ridden back toward the Bar C without taking any cattle to Amarillo. The men were tense, avoiding Colter whenever possible. His raging voice still echoed in their ears.

"Tom Matthews! That double-dealing, low-down, four-flushing rustler! He'll pay for this!"

With their heads lowered in shame the men had listened in silence to the Major's ravings.

After the raging passion had subsided and Colter had shut himself in the house they lounged around awaiting further orders, talking in low tones.

It was on the third morning that Colter confronted the men again. "I want ten of you men to accompany me to town. We're going to get the sheriff to swear all of you in as deputies. Get ready to ride."

It was mid-afternoon as the two riders rode across the range. Charlie was giving Riley the layout of the ranch and its boundaries. They crested a low hill and looked down to see a large group of horsemen moving swiftly across the valley.

"That's Major Colter and sheriff Metters! They're not out for a Sunday ride, Riley. It means trouble for Tom."

"Let's follow them aways, Charlie. I'm kind of interested in what they're up to."

They dropped off the hill and followed the racing riders. They had covered about eight miles when they saw the dust cloud in the distance.

Charlie's voice betrayed his excitement. "It's Tom and his men bringing back Bonnie's herd. When the Major closes in there'll be the devil to pay."

"Reckon we better pick up our pace then. I'd like to see the beginning of this."

As Riley and Charlie approached the sheriff's men who were now sitting their horses and facing Tom and his men they were just in time to catch Metters' words.

"All of you men are under arrest for rustling. These men with me have been given orders to shoot anyone resisting arrest. Unbuckle your gunbelts and let them fall."

"I reckon you got this all wrong, sheriff," spoke Tom. "As you can see we are bringing these cattle back to the Rocking D."

Charlie jumped his horse to Tom's side. "He's telling the truth, sheriff! You can't arrest Tom and his men. How are you gonna arrest men working for the Rocking D and herding their own cattle?"

Riley grinned as he watched the sheriff's face turn crimson. He gave Colter a quick glance. This was a fool's hand he was playing. Even the kid knew it.

"I don't recall Ms. Drake ever speaking of hiring these men. I'm taking them in for rustling. You get in my way, Charlie and I'll lock you up with them. I got a hankering to put you in jail anyhow." He motioned to the men with him.

"Alright, boys, collect their guns. I guess the cattle will have to remain here for the time being."

Riley nudged his horse a little closer. "Charlie and I will keep hazing them on their way, sheriff. We're both Rocking D hands."

Metters turned his horse and stepped it closer to Riley. His displeasure showed both in his eyes and voice. "I see you didn't take my advice, mister. You should have kept riding. If I don't miss my guess you're probably one of this bunch."

"Don't appear to be a rustling matter to me. At least not by the men with the cattle."

"I'm not interested in your opinions. I'll be keeping an eye on you." He turned his horse and stepped it to the side of Colter. "Let's get these men back to town."

Riley noticed the smile on Colter's lips as he looked at Tom. It was a dark smile that never reached his eyes.

"You ready to get these cattle moving again, Charlie?" Riley turned his horse back to the waiting herd.

"Coming, Riley." He gave Tom a quick glance before leaving his side. "Don't you be worrying, Tom. Bonnie will clear all this up."

It was night and the town was crowded as Bonnie and Riley rode down the beige, dusty street. The loud sounds of laughter and the dizzy notes from the pianos drifted out of the saloons.

"Looks like they're celebrating the capture of Tom and his men. Having quite a party tonight," spoke Riley lowly.

"Most of them are from the Bar C. I'd say the Major has more on his mind than a celebration. There will be a mob gathering shortly."

The two pulled up at the sheriff's office and dismounted, then walked inside.

Metters was sitting behind his desk in conversation with his deputy. His talking ceased abruptly as he turned his eyes to Bonnie. "Come in, Ms. Drake. I've been expecting you."

"I understand you have some of my men in jail, sheriff. The ones you caught with my cattle."

"That's right, ma'am. Tom Matthews and his band of cutthroat rustlers."

"Do you mind if I speak with him?"

Metters rose slowly to his feet, glancing from Bonnie to Riley. "I see no reason why not." He nodded his head toward Riley. "He'll have to wait out here. I still think he's one of Tom's men."

Bonnie followed Metters to the cells. She stood without speaking, waiting for him to leave her with the prisoners.

Metters hesitated, wanting to hear what she had to say. When she remained silent he scowled darkly and walked back to his office.

Tom stepped quickly to the cell door.

"I'm sorry, Tom. I was afraid something like this would happen."

"It's Colter's play, Ms. Drake. Him and that lousy sheriff of his."

Their conversation was interrupted by loud shouts and excited talk as men began gathering outside the saloons. A rough, hoarse voice rose above the crowd in an angry, slurring tone. "I say we oughta hang 'em! They've been running loose on the range too long."

His words brought a roar of agreement from the liquored crowd.

Colter stood just inside the saloon doors and watched with pleasure. Without turning his head he spoke lowly from the side of his mouth to Shep and Stu who were behind him. "Keep them drinking, boys. In another hour they'll be ready to tear the jail down and lynch Tom."

Tom and Bonnie listened intently to the mob outside. It was an ugly sound.

"I came to get you out. On one condition, that is."

"One condition?"

"Yes. That you and your men will agree to work for me for one year. You can be my foreman."

Tom shook his head and took a step backwards. "I don't know about that, Ms. Drake. The boys have been getting mighty restless lately and wanting to move on. They don't like being tied down to one place."

The voices outside grew in intensity. Someone fired a shot and it appeared to excite them even more as their yells grew louder. They had moved closer to the jail.

"That's a hanging crowd out there, Tom. Most of them are the Major's men."

"You drive a hard bargain, Ms. Drake."

"I have to. All I have is at stake."

"Okay, then, I'll stay put for one year but after that I'm a free man. You understand?"

Bonnie turned quickly and walked back inside the office. "I want my men released, sheriff."

Metters stood up quickly. "Hold on there, Ms. Drake. There's more to this than you know about. There was a man killed in that fracas out on the plains. Duke Clemmons. Besides, the

Major has three more men missing, supposedly dead."

"Duke Clemmons was the leader of the men who rustled my cattle, sheriff. As for the three missing men I suggest that the Major find their dead bodies, along with witnesses before he makes any accusations as to what happened to them. If Tom and his men are not released I'm sending a wire south requesting Ranger help up here."

"Now don't get so all doggone shook up, ma'am. I might release Tom and his men but I'll be wanting them around in case I need them for questioning."

"You can ride out to the ranch anytime you want to see them. When you come make sure the Major and his men are not with you. I'm not so fond of their company."

Metters spoke to Deputy Forbes who had been standing by silently and listening to their conversation. "Go get their horses and bring them around to the back. Make sure you're not seen." He turned back to Bonnie. "When you leave I'd be obliged if you would take the back streets. That crowd outside is all steamed up for trouble. I'll go over and have a chat with the Major and see if he can settle his boys down."

Bonnie and Riley stepped to the window and watched the mob drawing nearer as Metters went to release the prisoners.

As Tom buckled on his gun, Metters gave him a hard look. "You missed hanging this time but I wouldn't count on it the next go around. The boys won't be bringing you into town again. They'll hang you out on the range."

Tom settled his hat on his head. His eyes brightened as he spoke to Metters. "You make sure you're not with them when they try it. There'll be some who won't see the hanging, that is, if there is one."

The men walked quickly to the back door and stepped outside as Bonnie and Riley walked out the front.

Metters followed them outside. As they mounted and rode away he headed for the Silver Spur.

Little Charlie

Chapter Ten

Tom and Riley sat on the low hill and gave their horses a breather. There was no breeze blowing and sweat trickled slowly down their faces.

Tom looked at Riley through a thick cloud of smoke he had just exhaled. "I sent some of the boys after the rest of Ms. Drake's cattle. It was a fool play I made. I should never have tied in with Colter."

Riley studied Tom's face. He had seen a hundred others who had forked the wrong trail and fell in with the wrong crowd. Some never made it back. There were a few like Tom who managed to slip back across the line and stay on the right side of the law. He liked the big, rough Texan with the low slung gun.

He listened as Tom related to him the story of his family. He ended by talking about Charlie.

They continued to talk as they gouged their horses and descended the low hill. After crossing a shallow hollow they began the ascent of another hill when suddenly the air became filled with the angry whine of bullets as guns roared from the top of the ridge.

"Salt 'em down, boys!" The loud yell came from the crest of the hill.

Riley's horse was down and kicking out its last breath. He had managed to leap from it just in time.

Tom jerked his horse around to pick Riley up. He never finished his move. A bullet knocked him from the saddle. He rolled over twice and came up with his gun roaring and rocking hard against his palm. Another slug plowed across his scalp and he went down and out.

With his gun in his hand Riley lay still and looked from the corner of his eye at the hilltop. He saw two men rise slowly and then the head of a third.

"Keep your rifle trained on that new hand, Dago. We'll see if either one is still alive."

The two men stepped slowly and cautiously toward Riley.

Large beads of sweat covered Riley's face. He had to move. The men were drawing closer and he knew they would kill him where he lay. He estimated his chances. It was the one still on the hilltop that worried him. He had no choice. He leaped to his knees and began firing.

He saw one of the men double over as his bullet struck him in the midsection. It was all he saw for the bullet of the man on the hilltop struck him. It knocked him backwards and he hit the ground hard. He heard the faint shouts of the two men, then darkness washed over his eyes.

Charlie watched the big birds drop lower and rode in their direction. He and the men were out scouring the range for Tom and Riley. They hadn't come in last night.

He was still a hundred yards away when he glimpsed the bodies lying on the gently sloping hillside. He spurred his shaggy mustang and raced to their side.

Both their horses were dead. After checking their pulse he was satisfied they were still alive, yet barely. The ground beneath them was stained with dried blood. They had lost a lot, maybe too much.

He grabbed his rifle from its boot and quickly fired three successive shots into the air. After pausing a few seconds he repeated the action.

He jerked the canteen from his saddle and leaped to Tom's side. The bloody furrow along the side of his head was an ugly wound and swollen badly. As he worked over Tom's face with the wet kerchief he turned quickly at the sound of approaching horses.

It was Tap, Jed, and Kelly.

Tap leaped from his saddle and immediately took over the doctoring of Tom and Riley. "Kelly, you and Jed better fetch a wagon and the doctor. I'd send Charlie but I don't want him in town alone. I'll do what I can for them but they need a doctor's care."

Kelly and Jed turned their horses and raced away.

"They were ambushed! The dirty bushwhackers laid for them on that hilltop," spoke Charlie heatedly.

"That's the way it looks, Charlie. Maybe they're not done for yet though. Bring me my canteen, will you?"

Tap and Charlie stood to their feet after cleaning Tom and Riley's wounds.

"They're going to be okay, ain't they,

Tap?" Charlie's voice quivered slightly as he stared at the bodies lying silent and motionless.

"Depends on how much blood they've lost. They were hard hit. Let's mosey up there on the ridge and see if we can find anything."

An hour of searching turned up nothing except for indistinct marks upon the ground where the ambushers had waited. Tap sighed deeply in frustration as he turned to descend the hill.

"Someone's coming!" Charlie shielded his eyes against the glare of the falling sun.

"It's the boys coming with the doctor. Let's hurry back to Tom and Riley."

Jed leaped from his horse as he halted near Tap. "How they making it?"

"They're still breathing but that's about all."

Doc Sweezy climbed hurriedly from the wagon seat and bent over the bodies, examining them quickly but thoroughly. "Better get them loaded in the wagon quick, boys. They're in bad shape. Time is of essence here."

Tap opened the door to leave, then paused, looking back at Charlie. "You still have your gun?"

"Right here." Charlie lifted his shirt exposing the handle of the heavy forty-four stuck in his belt.

"Good. I'll be close by. Don't let anyone in this room unless it's someone you can trust. When Colter hears that they're still alive he'll make another attempt to kill them."

It was after supper when Doc Sweezy made another call on Tom and Riley. As Tap, Bonnie, and Charlie looked on, he bandaged their wounds again. "They're lucky to still be alive. The next three days will be crucial. They'll have spells of consciousness, then black out again. Don't be alarmed if they're delirious. They've got a fifty- fifty chance. I'll stop by again in the morning unless you send for me before then."

"Thank you, doctor," said Bonnie, her voice quivering. "Please do all you can for them."

"Don't worry, Ms. Drake. I work for Doctor Sweezy and am under no obligation to anyone else." He walked out of the room.

Charlie lay on the blanket which was spread in front of the door. He blinked his eyes against the sleepiness that was trying to close them.

The room was hot and stuffy and beads of sweat covered his face. He had locked the window and pulled the curtains.

It was close to midnight and Tom had been moving restlessly on his bed, uttering a mass of unintelligible words. His fever was high and his body drenched in sweat.

Riley's condition was hardly better. The doctor had been worried that the bullet may have nicked his lung at first for at times there were spots of fresh blood appearing at the corners of his mouth with tiny, frothy bubbles.

Suddenly Charlie's eyes opened wide. He cocked his ear and listened. Was that a faint creaking of a board he had heard in the hallway? He strained his ears and listened to see if the sound would come again. There! It was the faint creaking of someone stepping on a loose board again. He glanced at the window but saw nothing.

Someone was in the hallway slipping near the door. He wondered if Tap had heard it. He was in the opposite room from where he lay.

He picked up the heavy forty-four in both hands. He could feel the slow trickle of sweat running down his neck.

He knew the door couldn't be opened without a good bit of force for he was lying almost against it. Hardly daring to breathe he waited and listened.

Another quick glance at the window revealed nothing. There was no shadow showing. The moonlight would reveal any form that showed itself against the window pane. The curtains were beige and while he could see out it would be almost impossible for anyone to see inside the room.

A slight shudder ran across his body. There was suddenly something different about the room than there had been a few minutes ago. What was it? The door was still locked and no one had shown themselves against the window.

He silently rose to his feet and looked around the deeply shadowed room. The faint, cool draft of air felt good on his hot face and sweaty neck.

Nothing else moved and nothing stirred. The creaking in the hallway had ceased. He stood like a statute for three long minutes and, hearing nothing else lay back down.

Tom groaned again and uttered something about a shooting in Amarillo. A minute later he mumbled out the name Bonnie.

The room was becoming a little less

stuffy with the faint draft of air circulating and passing through it.

He glanced back at the window and saw the curtains rippling slightly. The tiny movements cast strange, mysterious shadows on the wall.

Suddenly he lifted the gun in his hands and pulled back the hammer as large beads of sweat popped out on his brow again. He leveled the gun at the window and began slowly searching every inch of the pane. It just dawned on him! The window had not been cracked or broken and he and Tap had made sure it had been locked. That faint draft of air and the tiny movements of the curtains--- what had caused them?

He saw it then. The faint shadow of part of a man's arm. In his hand was a gun and it was pointed in the direction of Tom's bed.

He aimed his gun at the shadowy wrist and pulled the trigger. There was a loud yelp of either fright or pain and afterwards something banged against the side of the building outside.

Almost immediately there came a loud banging on the door and Tap's voice. "Charlie! Charlie, are you okay?"

"I'm okay, Tap." Charlie kicked back his

blanket and opened the door.

"What happened?" Tap's roving eyes searched the room.

"Someone was fixing to take a sneak shot through the window. I think I winged him. If you happen to see anyone around with a winged gun hand you'll know he was the back-shooting varmit."

They walked to the window and looked through the shattered pane.

Tap ran his finger along the edges of one of the small frames. "Smart was what he was. Cut that pane out like it was nothing."

"He must've been quieter than a church mouse. I heard nothing at the window, just the creaking of a loose board in the hallway."

Tap pulled the curtains back in place. "There were probably two of them. I was listening to those creaking sounds in the hallway myself. It was just a ruse to draw attention away from the window."

Tap walked back to the door. "You did fine, Charlie. I'll go tell Maria that everything is okay and folks can go back to sleep. I think I'll mosey on outside and see if I can spot anything. I don't think there will be another attempt tonight." He stepped out the door.

Charlie locked the door and stepped quickly

to Tom's side. Tom was delirious. He continually groaned and mumbled.

Charlie felt a slight shadow of fear pass across his heart. He reached down and with the corner of the sheet wiped Tom's wet face as a mist covered his eyes. "Don't you ride out on me, Tom. I need you. You hear?"

He heard Maria and Tap voices down the hallway and then the sound of other voices. As he stepped back to the door and spread his blanket again the voices grew silent.

Tap walked slowly around the corner of the building and searched the ground carefully. He almost stepped on the gun lying partly concealed in the grass before he saw it.

He picked it up and examined it by the light of the moon. There was a small chip on the wooden handle. The piece was about an inch long and a half inch wide that was missing. It was an old chip but the blood on the handle was fresh.

He replaced the gun on the ground and returned to his room. He would be looking for that gun again but his greatest interest would be in the man wearing it.

Little Charlie

Chapter Eleven

It had been a week since Tom and Riley had arrived in town. Their wounds were now healing and they were itching to be up and around.

As Tap stepped into the room he was met by the smiling face of Charlie.

"Looks like they're on the mend, Tap. Doggone if ain't a wonder what some folks will do to get out of work."

"I think you're right, Charlie. I've seen men get shot and be herding cattle the next day." He smiled as he looked at Tom and Riley. "Take Tom and Riley here. They've been bedfast for a week. Makes a man wonder, it surely does. You reckon you could slip over to the hardware store without Godwin taking a shot at you? I need a couple of boxes of ammunition."

"Sure, Tap. If you hear gunfire though, you better come a running."

Riley chuckled and turned to face Tom. "It's good they've got us to look after. If they didn't have this job they would be out of one. They sure don't know nothing about cattle."

Charlie grunted lowly in pretended disgust, then walked out of the room.

The town was quiet as he opened the front door of Maria's and gave the street a quick scrutiny before stepping out on the boardwalk. It took only a minute until he was looking through the window at Godwin's store.

Mrs. Godwin was behind the counter waiting on a customer. Two other ladies were looking over a variety of articles scattered loosely on a table. He could not see any sign of Bert. He stepped inside.

Mrs. Godwin lifted her head at the sound of the opening and closing of the door. "Why, Charlie Matthews! I haven't seen much of you lately. Where have you been keeping yourself?"

Charlie smiled good-naturedly. "I'm working for the Rocking D now. I've got myself a regular cowhand job. Guess you heard about Tom and

Riley getting shot. I've been staying in town with them."

"Yes, I heard about that awful shooting. They still haven't found the men who did it, have they?"

"No, ma'am, but when Tom and Riley are able to get about I'd say they'll find the sneaking varmints."

"What can I get for you?"

"Tap sent me over for a couple of boxes of ammunition. Forty-fours."

She turned to the shelf behind her for the order and placed them on the counter. "Here they are. Anything else I can get for you?"

"I guess that will do it." He laid his money on the counter and stuffed the heavy boxes in his pockets. He was fixing to leave when one of the lady customers spoke to him.

"Young man, could you climb upon that stool and reach me one of those buckets?" She pointed to several buckets hanging on nails near the ceiling.

"Sure thing, ma'am. I'll have it for you in just a jiffy." He climbed upon the stool and stretched himself as high as his short frame would allow. He was barely able to touch the bottom of the bucket.

Charlie balanced himself on his tiptoes and

was able to get his fingertips under the bottom rim of the bucket. Slowly he began to slide the handle of the pail from the nail.

As the handle bumped across the nail head he lost his balance and the bucket came plunging down. It crashed upon the glass candy jar on the end of the counter. As the jar shattered and the bucket banged loudly on the floor the back door was thrown open and Bert leaped into the room.

"What in thunder is going on in here," shouted Bert excitedly. "Anyone hurt?"

"Everything is fine, Mr. Godwin, I believe," said the lady customer staring at Charlie on the floor. "Just a minor accident. This young man was trying to help me. He'll be lucky if he's not injured." She stepped closer to Charlie. "Are you okay, young man?"

"I think so," said Charlie, rising to his feet.

At the sound of the familiar voice Bert's face twisted in a dark frown and his fingers closed over the nearest thing at hand. An axe handle. With his eyes lit by a burning hatred and his face dark with malice he advanced upon Charlie.

"Charlie Matthews! I should have known. I'm going to whale the living daylights out of you! You've wrecked the place again."

"Hold on there, Bert! It wasn't my fault. You hung those doggone buckets so high that no one can reach them." He began backing up as he glanced for a way of escape. The front door was out of the question for Bert was even now blocking that exit. He'd have to try for the back door.

Suddenly Bert lunged forward and took a sweeping blow at Charlie with the axe handle. He missed by only inches but he caught the window pane which shattered under the heavy impact.

The broken window intensified Bert's anger. "I've changed my mind, you little varmit. I'm not going to only beat the daylights out of you but I'm going to break both your legs." His eyes were becoming bloodshot and the hair which was previously plastered to his head now lay fallen across his face.

As the lady customer watched Bert stalk Charlie and heard his evil threatenings she suddenly screamed. "Help! Help! Somebody get the sheriff. Quick! There's going to be a murder."

Hurried footsteps could be heard from outside as someone ran toward the sheriff's office.

Charlie waited until Bert circled away from the aisle leading to the back door. It was his only means of escape.

Thinking he had Charlie cornered, Bert's eyes lit with triumph. "Now, you little red-headed rooster, I've got you." He swung the axe handle again, this time missing the lady customer by a hair's breath.

"Bert Godwin! You nearly hit Mrs. Quinn. Put that axe handle down before you hurt someone," yelled Mrs. Godwin.

"Ah, but I do intend to hurt someone," replied Bert as he began grinning wolfishly. "I'm going to do Three Forks a great favor. I'm fixing to kill the greatest enemy this town's ever had."

Charlie saw his chance and leaped for the back door. It had no sooner slammed shut behind him than he heard the axe handle crash against it.

Bert grabbed the double-barrel shotgun from the rack and breaking it open fished two shells from the box lying near it. He quickly loaded the chambers and rushed for the back door with Mrs. Godwin clawing at his coattail.

He jerked the door open and spied Charlie nearing the door of the Silver Spur. He was running as fast as his short legs could carry him. He threw the gun to his shoulder and took careful aim. His finger tightened on the trigger.

At the same instant the hand of Mrs. Godwin came down hard on his arm.

The gun exploded.

As the glass shattered in the saloon window near him, Charlie hit the batwing doors, falling inside. As quick as a cat he leaped to his feet and saw Con Silvers pulling his sawed-off express gun from under the bar. He turned quickly and jumped back through the doors.

Immediately came the sound of the loud exploding gun from inside the saloon and he was showered with splinters from the doors.

Out of the corner of his eye, Charlie saw sheriff Metters high-tailing it out of town after an empty wagon pulled by two stampeding horses. The shotgun blast from Godwin had spooked the horses which were hitched to the supply wagon out back of the store.

A hissing sound made Charlie glance at the alley which separated the saloon from the hotel.

"Pssst-sstttt! Charlie!" The voice was low, whispering. "It's me, Bonnie. Quick. In here!"

Charlie darted inside the alley.

"Hurry! My horse is at the other end of the alley. You scat back to the ranch as fast as you can. I'll get me a horse at the stable and ride in later."

Bonnie waited until she heard the pounding hooves of the horse leaving on the backstreet and then stepped upon the boardwalk as a dozen men gathered in front of the saloon.

Con came rushing through the batwings and began looking up and down the street for Charlie. "Where'd that little weasel go?"

One of the men pointed toward the alley. "I think he ducked into that alley but there ain't no use looking. The way he was stepping, he's probably half way across Texas by now."

"Where's Metters?" Con's voice was filled with anger.

"He's chasing that runaway team Godwin spooked when he shot at Charlie," came another voice from the group. "I'd say he's nigh on to seven miles down the road by now."

A loud chuckling broke out among the men. Three Forks hadn't seen this much excitement in months.

Con glared at the laughing men and strode back inside.

"Wonder why they were after Charlie? He ain't such a bad lot," voiced one of the men.

"It's Bert's play," came a reply. "He hates the little fellow. He says that every time Charlie comes into his store something gets busted up."

"Well, boys, let's have a drink. I'll buy the first round." The speaker led the way inside the saloon, still chuckling.

Bonnie acquired a team and wagon and left the stable, heading for Maria's. After pulling close to the door, she jumped down and began straightening the blankets in the wagon bed. Satisfied, she walked inside.

Walking to Tom and Riley's room, she knocked then stepped inside.

"What in the deuce is going on out there," asked Tom, stepping close to her. "Someone rob the bank?"

"No, Tom. It was Bert Godwin and Con Silvers shooting at Charlie."

"Charlie! What in blazes for? He wasn't hurt, was he?"

"No, he should be half way back to the ranch by now. I slipped him away on my horse. Someone said he had an accident over at Bert's store and Bert got all out of sorts again."

"As soon as I'm able to ride I'll be back to have a chat with Mr. Bert. He's overdue for a good straightening out himself."

"Are you both ready to leave now?" Bonnie looked from one to the other.

"We're ready," said Riley. "I'll be glad to get out in the air again."

Tom and Riley groaned lowly as they laid down in the wagon bed and tried to make themselves comfortable.

Bonnie clicked the horses into motion and took the south trail out of town heading for the Rocking D.

Chapter Twelve

Tom and Riley were saddling their horses as Charlie pulled the supply wagon next to the porch. It had been two weeks and their wounds were healing. After drawing the cinches tight they led the horses to where Charlie was waiting.

"You sure you want to chance another trip to town, Charlie? Metters may try to lock you up." Riley laid the reins over his saddle.

"He ought to have Silvers and Godwin in jail. They tried to murder me. The next time I may decide to shoot back."

"You leave that gun tucked in your belt and out of sight. Riley and me are gonna have a word with those two. You're too young to be toting a hogleg and pistol fighting. You hear me, Charlie?" Tom's face portrayed both anger and concern.

The door opened and Bonnie stepped out on the porch. "Well, it's good to see you two up and stirring around. How are you feeling this morning?" She noted the softening of Tom's eyes as he looked at her and smiled in satisfaction.

"Fine as rabbit hair, Ms. Drake. Are you sure that you and Charlie will be safe going into town without one of the men?"

"We'll be fine, Tom. Besides, Lloyd is the only one on the ranch. The others are out with the cattle. With that last bunch they brought in we have close to two thousand head back on the range. I just don't know how to thank you."

"No need to, ma'am. It was my fault they were taken in the first place. Riley and me may tag along behind you later." He held out his hand to her and she climbed into the wagon seat.

Charlie clicked the horses into motion and the wagon rolled out of the yard.

"This is gonna hurt some." Riley started to swing himself into the saddle, then paused. "Looks like we've got company."

The horseman was riding a lineback dun and his pace was slow and easy.

Tom slipped the thong from his gun and began rolling a smoke as he watched the rider draw nearer.

The rider reined his horse in and stopped a few yards from where the two men stood. A faint smile touched his lips as he dismounted. "Howdy, Tom. Thought I would ride by and see if you could use another hand."

Tom suddenly recognized the face. "I remember now. You're Dorsky."

"Pete Dorsky. Yeah, I've been riding loose since Duke was killed. The Major decided he didn't need my services any longer. I didn't know if you all were taking on any new hands or not."

"I reckon we could take you on, Pete. Lloyd's in the barn. You can look him up and stay close around the ranch for a couple of days. It might be best to keep outa sight for a spell."

"Much obliged. I'll have a chat with Lloyd and see you later." He led his horse toward the barn.

Riley watched Pete walk away. "Was he one of the men who rustled Ms. Drake's cattle?"

"Yeah, he was there when Duke made his play and I killed him."

"I think I'd like to have a chat with him and Lloyd when we get back from town."

They climbed into their saddles and rode from the yard in the direction of Three Forks.

Bonnie and Charlie climbed to the wagon seat and headed back to the ranch. Their trip to town had been without incident.

It was midmorning and the sky was clear except for a few small clouds hanging over the distant mountain peak to the southwest.

Major Colter stood in the doorway of the Silver Spur and watched Bonnie and Charlie's departure. As they disappeared from view he walked back to the bar and whispered lowly to Silvers, then beckoned for his two lieutenants.

Shep and Stu finished their drinks quickly and followed Colter out the back door.

"Stu, slip through the alley and bring our horses. We've played around long enough with Bonnie Drake." He pulled his gun from the holster and checked the cylinder. It was fully loaded.

Moments later Stu returned leading the horses and they quickly raced out of town.

Two miles from Three Forks the trio turned sharply west and raced toward Running Water Creek. As they neared the crest of the low hill they dismounted and peered over the summit. They saw the wagon approaching slowly on the trail.

"We'll finish the job we started a few weeks ago. If that little coyote of a Charlie hadn't come along when he did she would have been pushing up grass by now. Shep... you and Stu take Charlie. I'll take Ms. Drake myself."

Colter slapped at a pesty fly as the wagon drew nearer. "When these two are out of the way you boys can remove Tom and Riley. The rest of the men will drift when they're gone."

Shep nestled the rifle against his shoulder. "You reckon Metters will hold out? He's not been looking too happy lately."

"He will if he knows what's good for him. He's in this as deep as we are. If he decides he wants out later we'll bury him along with the rest."

The wagon was almost directly below them. They removed their hats and snuggled their rifles tightly against their shoulders.

Charlie gave a quick glance at the hilltop as

they approached the place where he had found Bonnie lying hurt by the trail. Suddenly his eyes widened and he started to yell. Too late!

The bullet knocked him backwards off the seat a split second before the loud explosion was heard.

Stu's bullet followed along behind Shep's but the knocking of Charlie from the wagon seat made it miss. The bullet dug into the seat where he had been sitting.

The horses bolted at the sudden blast of the rifles and Bonnie was jerked backwards. It was what saved her life for the bullet from Colter's rifle only grazed her forearm instead of lodging in her exposed side.

Bonnie clutched the back of the seat with her other hand to keep from being thrown from the bouncing wagon. The team was running madly and just a few feet from the embankment.

Again the rifles cracked from the hilltop and splinters jumped from the wagon seat.

Bonnie jerked violently in sudden pain. At the same instant one of the wagon wheels struck a small rock and the wagon swayed dangerously on two wheels.

Bonnie screamed as she felt the wagon toppling. She jerked hard on the reins.

Little Charlie

The stampeding horses felt the weight of the wagon and tried to swerve away from the embankment. Their efforts were futile.

As the wagon spilled over the bank with a loud, splintering crash, Bonnie leaped from the seat.

The horses screamed and kicked savagely as they were jerked over the embankment and hit the ground.

From the hilltop the three men looked on with satisfaction. They could see the small body of Charlie lying sprawled and unmoving on the ground below. His head and face were covered with blood.

The dust settled and they saw Bonnie lying several feet from the shattered wagon. She could never have survived the shooting and the toppled wagon.

The horses were still down, bound by the weight of the wagon on the lines and one was suffering from a broken leg.

"Let's ride, men. We'll slip back into town. Stu, when we get back slip our horses back through the alley and tie them out front. As far as anyone's concerned we've been in Con's back room playing poker."

Riley pulled his horse to a sudden stop and

looked up the trail.

"What's wrong?" Tom jerked his horse to a halt and listened intently, watching Riley's eyes.

"I thought I heard rifle fire. Sounded like it was up ahead."

"That's our direction. Let's hope it doesn't mean more trouble for Bonnie and Charlie."

They spurred their horses and raced ahead.

They were two hundred feet away when they saw the body of Charlie.

"Charlie!" Tom yelled as he spurred his horse savagely.

Riley was only a second behind. As Tom rushed by the overturned wagon, he leaped from his horse and jumped down the embankment to where Bonnie lay.

"He's still alive, Riley," yelled Tom as he bent over Charlie.

"Ms. Drake's alive too. She needs a doctor though. She may have some broken bones."

Suddenly Tom lifted his head and looked down the trail leading toward town. "Riley! Someone's coming."

Riley stood quickly to his feet. "Let's get out of sight. We might learn something if we're not seen."

Riley retrieved their horses and led them quickly behind a small cluster of trees.

Tom stepped behind a rock near the trail and hunkered down within twenty-five feet of Charlie's body. He peered around the rock and saw the rider coming. "It's Metters. I can see his badge."

"Let him ride on in. He may have been in on this himself. He's got the makings for it." Riley cupped his hands over the horses' nostrils to keep them quiet.

Metters saw the body and leaped from the saddle. He gave a quick, searching glance around and ran to Charlie's side. He lifted the small head in his left hand and began wiping away the dirt from his face.

After making sure he was still breathing he ran to get his canteen. As he sponged the young, soft face he let a few drops fall into his eyes and mouth. "Charlie! Charlie, boy! Can you hear me?"

Charlie's head moved and his eyes blinked slowly open. He coughed out the few drops of water that threatened to strangle him. His vision was blurred as he looked into Metters' face. "Is that… you… sheriff? Where… am I?"

"It's okay, Charlie. This is Metters. You're gonna be okay. Can you tell me what happened?"

He tried to speak but his head was

spinning and he still couldn't see clearly. His words came as broken fragments, yet they were understood. "Ma..jor Col..ter. His two…men." his eyes rolled back and he sank into unconsciousness.

"Major Colter!" A grim expression covered Metters' face as he said the name loudly.

Tom stepped out from behind the rock. His eyes burned with a fire of vengeance. When he spoke his words were sharp. "I reckon we both heard right, sheriff."

Metters spun around, his hand dropping for his gun. It froze as he looked into Tom's eyes. "Don't you be going off half-cocked, Tom. Charlie needs a doctor and I'm sure Ms. Drake will too if she's still alive. I'll ride back to town for Doc Sweezy."

"Ms. Drake is alive. I can settle with Colter later. Don't get in my way when I come for him. If either Charlie or Ms. Drake dies I'm gonna kill three men. Don't make it four."

Without responding to Tom's words, Metters leaped into his saddle and raced back in the direction of town. As he spurred his horse he kept remembering the look in Tom's eyes and the cutting edge of his words. He shuddered slightly. He was as brave as the next man but Tom had meant what he said. The Major hadn't taken enough precaution this time. He was in big trouble. Besides, there was Riley who would b siding Tom. There was something about the cool, steady way he carried himself that spoke of more than a regular cowhand. If Riley wasn't a gunfighter he was badly mistaken. The Major's two aces might not be able to shoot him out of this trouble. With his mind filled with troubling thoughts he raced on to town.

As the doctor walked from the back room and stepped into the front office, Tom and Riley stood to their feet.

"How are they, doc?" There was a slight trace of fear in Tom's voice.

"Oh, they should be okay in a week or so. Ms. Drake is suffering from multiple bruises and has one broken rib. The bullet wound on her forearm wasn't much more than a graze. Charlie will be suffering headaches for a spell but he'll make out. I don't know who your enemies are but they mean business. These shootings are serious matters. If they don't stop soon someone's gonna wind up dead."

"Much obliged for your care of them.

You're right about one thing… somebody's fixing to wind up dead and I'm pretty sure who some of them are gonna be." Tom settled his hat on his head and glanced at Riley. "Let's go have a chat with Metters."

Metters and his deputy were preparing to leave for dinner when Tom and Riley walked through the door.

"Tom, Riley. Glad you stopped in. How's Charlie and Ms. Drake?"

"The doc says they are gonna be okay. I can't say the same for the ones who shot them."

Metters dropped his eyes from the piercing gaze of Tom. "I wanted to talk to you about that. Judge Tombs is expected in town on the evening stage. I've already talked with the Major and his two men. We're going to have a hearing set for in the morning if the judge don't object. How's that set with you men?"

Tom glanced at Riley. "We'll be here. Make sure Colter shows up."

"Like I said, I've talked to them. They promised to be here."

Tom looked at Riley. "You ready to go?"

"Ready and waiting." He followed Tom out the door.

"What do you think about that? Reckon Metters is on the level," asked Tom?

"It's more than I figured he would do. It could turn out to be a right interesting meeting. Do you know Judge Tombs?"

"Heard of him. They say he shoots right down the middle."

Riley rubbed his stomach. "I hope so. Let's get some dinner. My belly's already gnawing on my backbone."

They walked to Maria's and stepped inside. Behind them followed Metters and Forbes but when they saw them enter Maria's they changed direction and headed for the hotel.

Little Charlie

Chapter Thirteen

Three Forks was bustling with activity and excited conversations. It was the morning of the hearing. Bar C horses lined the hitching rails. The hearing had been set for ten o'clock. After breakfast at Maria's, Tom and Riley went to see Bonnie and Charlie who were staying in the back quarters of the doctor's office.

They stepped into the patients' room and were amazed to find the two sitting up and talking.

Charlie's head was bandaged but his vision had cleared and most of his dizziness was gone. Bonnie's brow was pinched in pain from the broken rib. When she moved she groaned lowly.

Tom's eyes were soft and his voice

shaky as he spoke to her. "How're you feeling, Ms. Drake?"

"I just hurt when I breathe. It feels like everything inside me has been shaken loose. I never knew that I had so many places that could hurt."

"I sure am sorry. As a rule Texas men are a good lot. Some are a bit rough around the edges but for the most part, a good lot. Every once in awhile a snake comes up out of the crowd. I reckon it's up to the rest of us to smash it when it does."

"Oh, Tom, please don't kill anyone! You know where Metters stands. He'd like nothing better than to pin a murder on you so he could send you to prison."

"Well, personally, ma'am, I think he's one of the snakes that need stamping out. As long as he and the Major are left running loose you and Charlie ain't gonna be safe at all."

"What about the hearing this morning? Doctor Sweezy said that Judge Tombs was in town and a hearing was scheduled for ten o'clock."

"We're on our way there now. The Major's had plenty of time to come up with an alibi. He's got twenty men who will swear

Little Charlie

he was somewhere else when the shooting took place."

"But Charlie said he saw them!"

"He will make Charlie out to be only a fool boy who was seeing things."

"I did see them, Tom!" Charlie's voice was filled with anger. "They were on the hilltop with only their heads showing. It was the Major and those two gunhands of his."

"I know, Charlie. Riley and I are gonna be sitting in at the hearing. You both just take it easy. Whether they jail the Major or not makes no difference. His days in Three Forks are numbered."

There was a tenderness in Bonnie's voice as she looked worriedly at Tom. "You be careful. I don't know what Charlie and I would do without you."

"We'll check back on you two later. We best be getting over to the saloon."

As Tom and Riley stepped through the saloon doors they were met with hard and challenging eyes. There was no sitting room so they stood close to the doors.

In front and facing the table where Judge Tombs sat was the Major and his two men. Sheriff Metters stood a little off to the side of the Judge. As Tom and Riley's eyes fastened on him he cast a nervous glance at Colter.

"Call this meeting to order, sheriff! I've got to catch the three o'clock stage to Santa Fe," ordered Tombs.

Metters stepped forward and called the meeting to order.

"Okay, Mr. Colter, what have you got to say?" Tombs piercing eyes fell on Colter.

"It's like this, your honor," spoke Colter as he stood to his feet. "This whole affair is a set-up by persons prejudiced against me. I have two witnesses who can swear to my whereabouts during the time of the shooting. My men and I were nowhere around Running Water Creek when the ambush took place."

"These two witnesses. Are they in this room?"

"Of course. They are Dago Williams and Matt Brown."

Tombs looked over the crowd and searched the faces of the men. His eyes lingered for a long moment on Tom and Riley. "Okay, Mr. Williams and Mr. Brown.. Step up here if you're in the room."

At the name of Dago the eyes of Tom and Riley brightened. A yellow gleam rose up in Riley's eyes as he watched the two men step forward. He remembered the name on the hilltop when he and Tom were ambushed. He calculated that Matt Brown would no doubt be one of the other two. He noted the place they had stepped from and saw a third man he assumed to be their partner.

Tom's face darkened with anger as he listened to the two men swear their lies. He had expected as much but inside the seething passion was rising dangerously.

After hearing Metters' account of finding Charlie and how he uttered a few delirious words in his moments of consciousness, Judge Tombs sat staring at the three smiling faces of the defendants. "I'm not so sure you men are as innocent as it appears. Personally, I think this whole thing has a bad smell. As a Judge I cannot operate on my own personal feelings but must adhere to the evidence presented. I cannot order you to be held." He looked at Metters. "Sheriff, I think this case bears further investigation. It's a reproach and stink upon Texas when women and children are not safe on the trails. I'm depending on you to extend this investigation."

"Sure, your honor. My deputy and I will find the ones responsible. You can count on it."

"This hearing is closed." Tombs stood to his feet and walked out of the saloon.

"The drinks are on me, boys!" The Major's voice rose above the loud talk and laughter. "Everyone belly up to the bar. If there isn't enough room we will pass a couple of bottles around."

As the crowd began to disperse, Tap stepped into the saloon and joined Tom and Riley.

"We may as well have a drink while we're here," spoke Tom lowly.

The three walked to the bar and ordered three drinks. Tom threw his money on the bar.

"The drinks are on the Major, boys. You can keep your money." Silvers pushed Tom's money back.

"We prefer to drink on ourselves, Silvers. We're kinda particular who we have a drink on." Tom's voice was sharp and hard.

"Suit yourselves. It's a free country." He picked up the money and began pouring more drinks.

"We aim to do just that. Suit ourselves, that is." Tom turned to face the room.

Suddenly Tap's eyes fell and rested on a holstered gun. On the outside handle there was a small chip. Recalling the night he had seen that gun and laid it back on the ground brought the old fighting fury rising inside. "You!" He pointed his forefinger at the man wearing the gun. "You seem to be favoring your wrist a mite. Perhaps you got it hurt a few nights ago, uh?"

"What's it to you, mister," came the response.

"A certain fellow tried to sneak a shot through the window at Maria's the other night."

"What's that supposed to mean to me. You trying to say something or do you just like to hear yourself talk?" He smiled nervously at the men standing near him.

A stillness crept through the room as the two men faced each other. Hands were frozen with drinks in them, halfway to their lips.

Shep and Stu set their glasses back on the bar and let their hands fall loosely to their sides, dangling close to their guns.

"I'll tell you what it has to do with it. Whoever tried that sneak shot got winged before they were able to get a shot off. They dropped their gun and ran away before picking it up. That gun had a chip on the handle. It favored the one you're carrying. I left it on the ground thinking its owner might return for it. I reckon he did."

Little Charlie

The man wet his dry lips with a darting tongue and glanced nervously around. The soreness wasn't completely gone from his wrist. It was still stiff and by the looks of the man he was facing he would need to be quick. He forced a hollow laugh and looked around again at the men watching. "Well, boys, looks like this stranger is full of tall tales. What'da you say we all have another drink?" He made as if to turn and his hand closed over his gunbutt.

Tap saw the move and was ready. He waited until the man's hand was lifting his gun out of the holster.

With a wolfish sneer on his face, Will Trumpet uttered a low whine. As he drew his gun he turned back to face Tap. His gun was rising when he saw Tap's hand move.

Tap palmed his forty-four with flashing speed and let go with two shots. One bullet struck Will's shirt pocket and the other plucked the second button from his shirt front, driving it deep inside.

As Will slowly fell his gun dropped from his nerveless and lifeless fingers.

Tap stared at the men watching. "Look at his wrist. If he hasn't got a bullet burn somewhere on it, I'm lying."

One of the bystanders stooped down and

lifted Will's limp hand. Across the top of his wrist was burned a small, narrow furrow that was still red. He lifted his eyes to look at Tap. "Looks like you called it right, mister. He drew first but that might not make much difference to his friends."

Suddenly Shep and Stu stepped out to face Tap. Their faces were set hard and their gun hands ready.

"Now, now, boys, hold it!" Major Colter held up a bottle. "I'm buying one more round before we ride. Shep! Stu! Let's have that drink. Now!"

For a full minute the two gunmen faced Tap who stood unwavering before them.

Colter's eyes were on Tom and Riley. They were ready to draw. The timing was not right. Perhaps soon he would unleash his two gunmen and lay Tom and Riley in their graves.

A faint smile touched the corners of Shep's lips as he stared at Tap. The smile never went any further. His eyes remained cold, flat, and calculating.

Tom's eyes remained on the two gunmen until they turned back to the bar. He had never seen them in action but judged them to be fast. Very fast.

Little Charlie

Chapter Fourteen

It was on the night of the hearing that the Rocking D hands were gathered in the bunkhouse smoking after their late supper.

Riley decided that now would be a good time to have a talk with Lloyd and Pete. He walked across the room to where they were sitting at a table. "I'd like to have a chat with you men if you will. Outside if you don't mind."

Pete gave Lloyd a quick glance. "Sure, Riley. I need some fresh air anyway."

The three men walked to the corral and leaned against the posts. After over an hour in deep conversation they started back to the bunkhouse.

Riley paused outside the door. "I'd be

obliged if you men didn't mention any of this to anyone for a few days."

"Whatever you say. You won't be hearing any of it repeated," replied Lloyd.

The next morning as the men saddled up to head out on the range, Riley led his horse to join Tom. "I'd like to ride into town this morning. I've got some business to attend to."

"If it's trouble I can ride along with you." Tom finished tightening the cinch.

"No trouble. It shouldn't take me long. I'll try to be back by early afternoon."

"Take as long as you need. I'll be close around unless something comes up. If you don't mind, ask the doctor when we can bring Charlie and Bonnie back to the ranch. I don't like them being in town any longer than they have to."

"Be glad to." Riley climbed into the saddle. "I'll see you later." He rode from the yard.

Riley pulled in at the Longhorn saloon and dismounted. He stepped inside and walked to the bar. After ordering a drink he selected a table near the window and sat down, watching the activity on the street.

He had been sitting for a half hour when he saw Deputy Forbes crossing the street in his direction. He rose quickly and walked to the door. As Forbes approached the saloon door, Riley stopped him. "Morning, deputy."

"Morning, Riley."

"I'd like to have a talk with you if you have a minute."

"Sure." Forbes stepped in the saloon. "What's on your mind?"

"Let's have a seat and I'll tell you about it." He ordered Forbes a drink and led the way to his table.

"What I'm fixing to say is confidential. I wouldn't want it spread around just yet. It will all come out soon enough. I've been asking a few questions about you. You seem to be a straight shooter and most folks cotton to you."

Forbes grew still and cautious as he listened to Riley's words.

"Three Forks is going to need a new sheriff soon. Hopefully you will be that man if you care for the job. Metters is on his way out."

Forbes shook his head in consternation. "What about the Major? He's the one that gets the sheriff elected."

"He's not going to be around much longer

either. Three Forks is a good town. It's got some poison weeds in it but they're fixing to be pulled. You interested or not?"

"Of course. That is… if it's on the level. What do you want me to do?"

"I want you to have a drink with Dago and Matt the next time they're in town. Have more than one if you need to. I know they lied to Judge Tombs but I want you to confirm it for me. They'll be wanting to brag about it. I'll be back in town tomorrow evening."

"They'll be in tonight. Most of the Bar C will. I'll see what I can do."

"Much obliged, Forbes. I'm counting on you."

The next morning Riley prepared to ride into town again. Pete and Lloyd accompanied him.

The back streets were deserted as the three rode to the back of the Longhorn saloon and dismounted. They slipped through the alley and entered the saloon through the side door.

After making sure there were no Bar C riders present they walked on to the bar.

Pete O'Malley paused in swiping the bar with his rag and looked curiously at the men.

"I've got a favor to ask of you, Pete," said

Riley.

"What'da you need?" He gave Pete and Lloyd a quick glance.

"I need a room where I can have some privacy for a couple of hours. I'll be having a meeting going on and don't want to be disturbed. There'll be four of us."

"You can use my office in the back if you like. I'll take a bottle and some glasses back there now." He smiled. "What'da you aiming on doing? Running for sheriff?"

Riley chuckled. "Maybe that wouldn't be such a bad idea. You think I might have a chance of winning?"

"To be honest with you, no, but I'd vote for you anyhow."

Riley spoke to Lloyd and Dorsky. "You two can go on back with Pete. I'll join you in a little bit."

Riley walked back to his table and took a seat where he could watch out the window again.

A few minutes later he was joined by Deputy Forbes. After a few whispered words they walked to Pete's office.

As Riley walked out of the doctor's office he saw two Bar C hands riding into town.

Instead of going to the saloon he watched as they rode on to Dobb's stable and dismounted. They opened the door and led their horses inside.

Riley pulled his hat a little lower on his forehead and, slipping the thong from his gun walked toward the stable.

Dago and Matt had just put their horses up and were turning to leave when Riley stepped inside.

"Saw you men ride in. I'd like to have a talk with you."

Their hands moved closer to their guns and dark frowns spread across their faces as they stared inquisitively at Riley.
"Whatever you've got to say make it quick," said Dago. "We're thirsty."

"I wouldn't worry too much about drinking right now, boys. You've got bigger problems than a thirst for whiskey."

"Are you gonna talk in riddles or what," replied Dago impatiently? They stepped apart and glared at Riley.

"I reckon you men know what perjury is. It can carry a pretty long sentence if a judge is so minded. You lied at Colter's hearing. I've got a sworn statement that you men weren't in the saloon playing poker when

Ms. Drake and Charlie were ambushed. Neither was Colter or his two gunnies."

"You're lying, Riley. Even if what you say is true, what can you do about it?"

"I can do plenty." Riley pulled back the left side of his vest which revealed his Ranger's badge. "You see, boys, you won't be held by Metters. You'll be in my custody. I'll take your guns now. Just unbuckle 'em and let 'em fall."

"You're loco! We ain't going to no jail. If we kill you we will swear you tried to jump us in here." Dago smiled wickedly. "I'm afraid you made a bad mistake, Riley. You should have stayed south. The only place you're going now is west. You know… like the evening sun." He went for his gun.

Matt saw the blurring movement. It was hardly more than a flashing streak as Riley's hand moved. It was the same movement other men had seen and what had made Riley a legend in most parts of Texas and points west. There were a total of seventeen men down his back trail that had faced that same draw and it had been the last thing they ever saw.

Dago and Matt made the same mistake.

Dago's gun was out of the holster when the impact of the bullet knocked him backwards against the stall.

Matt caught the second one. The red hot slug tore through his heart and left him standing with his gun held limply in his fingers. He started to speak but his words were only hoarse, raspy groans. He fell face forward and was dead when he hit the ground.

Riley heard loud shouts out on the street and a moment later Metters rushed into the stable.

Metters stared at the dead bodies of Dago and Matt, then turned to face Riley. "This can go hard on you, Riley."

Riley returned Metters' stare and spoke softly. "I'm a witness that they drew first. Have you got another one that can swear different?" The words were challenging, hard, pointed, and precise.

Metters hesitated and then declined the argument as men stepped up behind him. He turned to face them. "Alright boys, break it up and get about your business. This looks like a case of self-defense."

Two hours later Riley rode into the yard of the Rocking D. He was met by Tom who walked out to meet him.

"I'd say by the look on your face you've had

trouble." Tom studied the serious expression in Riley's eyes.

"Nothing to speak of," replied Riley as he dismounted and stripped the saddle from his horse. He turned it into the corral. "Two of those ambushers who laid for us got themselves killed this afternoon."

"Dago and Matt?"

"The same. I need to have a talk with you, Tom. There's something I reckon you ought to know."

"Let's have a seat on the porch then."

Riley rolled himself a smoke and handed Tom the makings. "I'm a Texas Ranger. I came to Three Forks to investigate the rustlings and killings up here. My orders were to look into the affairs of Major Colters, The Rocking D, and a man by the name of Tom Matthews. I think I've seen about enough. I've got sworn statements from Dorsky, Lloyd, and Deputy Forbes against Colter and his two men. Those statements also incriminate Metters. I'll be riding back into town in the morning. I'm taking Colter, Shep, Stu and Metters back with me. You still planning on riding in to get Ms. Drake and Charlie?"

"Yeah, I'm riding in for them. I reckon you know as well as anyone I rustled those cattle of Ms. Drake."

"I also know you brought them back. It's not for me to make such decisions but I judge a man for what he is... not for what he used to be. A man could do well on this ranch, especially if Colter was to be removed from the range. Besides... there's a certain small redhead that needs a brother's attention. I wouldn't want to deprive him of that."

Riley's words touched Tom deeply. He could have counted on two fingers the people who had ever spoken such words to him. Both were dead. "I'll have the boys ready to ride in the morning." He flicked his wasted cigarette into the yard.

"Let them stay here. I'm much obliged but I wouldn't want to see any more Rocking D hands killed." He stood slowly to his feet and stepped off the porch, heading toward the bunkhouse. As he walked across the yard he pondered over tomorrow and wondered if this would be his last trail. He would be facing the guns of Shep and Stu. They were reported to be fast. Very fast.

Tom stared after Riley until he disappeared inside the bunkhouse. He liked the tall Texan with the soft, drawling voice. One thing was for sure. He would be needing someone to stand with him tomorrow. He closed his eyes and contemplated over the situation. When Colter received the news that Riley was a Ranger he would become a desperate man and desperate men are dangerous men.

Little Charlie

Chapter Fifteen

It was early morning. The sun was just creeping up over the distant hilltop and casting a yellow hue upon the plains that lay still, wide, and open. The ranch was empty except for the two men who sat upon the wagon seat with the saddled horse tied behind.

Riley took a long look around the ranch and sighed deeply. "Gives a man kind of a lonely feeling. A fellow could get attached here if he wasn't careful."

There was deep emotion in Tom's tone of voice when he spoke. "I'm doggone sorry about you having to leave. Won't hardly be the same around here without you."

"It's my job, Tom. Always moving. Well, we best be riding. It's favoring a hot day and if I don't miss my guess it will get hotter before the sun goes down."

Little Charlie

Charlie stood at the window, his roving eyes searching the street below. "Wonder what Tap and the boys are doing in town, Bonnie? I've been watching them ride in by two's and three's for the last half hour. Something's coming off today. I can feel it in my bones. I haven't spotted Tom and Riley."

As he continued his vigil he saw Major Colter and his two lieutenants coming down the street at a shambling trot.

Colter sat his saddle like a cavalry officer, his blue-grey uniform spotless and the buttons shimmering in the sunlight. He pulled in at the Silver Spur and dismounted. After dusting himself off he led the way inside.

Before entering the doors Shep and Stu gave the street another careful scrutiny. Satisfied that all was well, they stepped inside.

Charlie's eye caught the movement across the street in the alley beside the Longhorn. There was a man concealed there with a rifle.

With his searching eyes running over the dusty street and the false-fronted buildings he saw another man down the street by Godwin's store. He was leaning against a post and smoking. It was another one of Tom's men.

Charlie walked over to his bed and lifted the heavy forty-four from under the pillow. After checking to make sure it was fully loaded he tucked it into his belt with his shirt tail concealing it.

Bonnie had been watching him curiously. "Charlie, what are you doing? What's going on outside?"

"I'm not sure, Bonnie. Your men are out in full force. I've been watching them position themselves all along the street. I'm fixing to go take a look. I still haven't seen Tom or Riley."

Bonnie stood to her feet. "Don't you dare go out there, Charlie! You might get killed!"

"I'm just going to slip around and take a look. No one will even know I'm around." He left the doctor's office by the back door and quickly stepped into the alley. It would shadow him enough to get close to the street and see what was taking place.

He heard the sound of more horses coming down the street and peered from the shadowed alley. The riders were from the Bar C and there were three of them. He watched as they jerked their horses to a halt as a low voice spoke from an alley near them. The words of the speaker were inaudible to his ears but the three riders looked to be angry and complaining.

As he continued to watch, the three men dismounted and sat down on a bench under the awning. He could see their dark frowns clearly.

Suddenly a wagon loomed into view. The creaking of its wheels sounded loud in the morning stillness. It was Tom and Riley.

A dog barked up the street and he could hear the stamping of the horses in the stables.

As Tom stopped the wagon in front of the doctor's office, Charlie remained still and watchful. His eyes widened when Tom and Riley began walking slowly toward the Silver Spur. He turned and hurried back through the alley and on to the rear of the saloon. After making sure he was unseen he slipped through the back door and moved cautiously toward the front. He stopped at the shadowed end of the long bar where he hunkered down and watched intently.

He was just beginning to catch his breath regularly when the batwing doors were pushed open and Tom and Riley walked inside.

The saloon was empty except for the Major, his two men and Con Silvers who was behind the bar polishing glasses.

Shep and Stu sat at the table with Colter. When their attention was drawn to the entrance of Tom and Riley, Charlie moved.

He soft-footed it to a position where he could watch the bar and not be seen. He drew the heavy pistol from his belt and gripped it tightly in both hands.

Riley led the way to Colter's table and stopped within six paces of the staring men. "Mawning, gents." His voice was soft, low, and drawling.

"Morning, Riley, Tom. What can I do for you?" Colter leaned back in his chair to a more comfortable position.

"For starters you all can keep your hands on the table where I can see them."

The thick, broad shoulders of Shep began bunching around his short, bulldog neck. The veins began swelling, turning darker, and his eyes turned into two sharp, piercing daggers. The hands that were wide and flat across the knuckles turned whiter as he gripped the glass of whiskey and stared at Riley.

Stu sat taking it all in calmly and quietly. He swallowed the mouthful of burning whiskey that he had been holding since Riley first spoke, then set the glass on the table. His big adam's apple bobbed twice and then seemed to lodge in place and remain still. His bird-like eyes became flat and emotionless. He waited like a deadly snake, still and silent.

After regaining his composure, Colter replied with a sharp, commanding voice. "Say what's on your mind and get out of here. You're beginning to annoy me."

"Let me handle this meddling stranger, Major!" Shep spoke through his wide, crooked teeth. "This is my line of work."

Riley smiled faintly. "Not stranger, Shep. Ranger! You men are under arrest."

"Ranger!" Stu straightened suddenly in his chair. "Well, Mr. Ranger, I hope you enjoyed your ride into town this morning. I'd say it was your last one."

The two gunmen rose slowly to their feet, their eyes burning with the lust to kill. To destroy these two opponents who stood before them.

Silvers listened intently to the conversation in silence. Large beads of sweat appeared on his face and began running down to his chin. He blinked his eyes against the salty drops, seemingly unable to lift his hand and wipe away the trickles.

Tom stood facing Stu with his big hand

hanging loosely by his gun. He watched the bird eyes, knowing they would give the signal of the gunman's intentions to draw. Then it came!

Stu's eyes lightened, giving them an instant clarity and the hand picked up the signal. It moved like a weaver's shuttle.

Shep's movement was simultaneous to that of Stu. His hand flashed like a darting snake's head. No sooner had his palm slapped his gunbutt than the weapon leaped from its holster, ready to spout forth its deadly fire.

In a fraction of a second four guns were roaring. As suddenly as it began it was over. Nine shots had been fired and the table and the floor were stained with blood. Tom's arm and side were bleeding but he was still on his feet. His shirt was becoming soaked with blood.

Stu was down and dead. One bullet had torn a hole through his heart and another had ripped through his throat. His eyes were wide-open, staring unseeing at the ceiling.

Riley stood with the hammer eared back on his forty-five, his eyes glued to Shep who had slumped down in his chair. He was alive and still wanting to kill. He had plenty of fight left in him. The two slugs through his chest had slowed him down but in no way had rendered him helpless.

Riley's right leg was wet with blood. It was quivering as he shifted his weight to his other leg.

Shep reached out with his left hand and took the half-full glass of whiskey from the table. He tossed off its contents. A shallow cough followed and small, bubbly drops of blood stained the corners of his mouth. "Ah, what the heck." He lifted his gun again.

Another bullet from Riley's gun cut through his chest and he toppled backwards out of his chair. His gun exploded twice as his finger pulled the trigger by reflex, shattering an overhead lamp and the front window pane.

Colter sat unmoving, unable to believe what his eyes had witnessed. His right arm was bleeding and his gun lay on the floor beside his chair.

Suddenly their attention was diverted to the bar as they heard Charlie's voice on the heels of his cocking pistol. "Go right ahead, Mr. Silvers. You might make it. I'm not nigh as good with a gun as Tom and Riley but neither are you."

Con slowly lowered the express gun to its place beneath the bar.

"You can step out from behind the bar

now," added Charlie. "Just step over there and have a seat with the Major."

Silvers had hardly settled in his chair when the doors were thrown open and Metters entered. Deputy Forbes was only a step behind him.

"What in the thunder happened in here," he asked as he walked quickly toward the men? His face darkened in anger as he stared at Colter holding his wounded arm and Shep and Stu lying dead on the floor. He faced Tom and Riley. "I'm putting you two men under arrest. You'll hang for this little party." He reached for his gun but it was jerked from its holster by Forbes.

"Sorry, sheriff, but I don't think you'll be needing this anymore." Forbes tucked the gun in his belt and turned to Riley. "What now, Ranger Riley?"

"Ranger! Well, why didn't someone tell me?" Metters' voice lost its anger and took on a more congenial tone.

Riley grinned at Metters. "Take the sheriff and the Major to the jail and lock them up, Forbes. We'll send the doctor over in a little bit."

Forbes motioned with his gun. "Okay, Major, let's go. You too, sheriff. Today's clean-up day for Three Forks."

As Forbes started the pair across the room he was stopped by Riley.

"Just a minute, Forbes. Take Silvers here with you. I think we're going to close down the Silver Spur temporarily. As soon as we find a new owner we'll open it again."

Tom's eyes softened as he looked over at Charlie. "Obliged for your help, Charlie. You wouldn't really have plugged Silvers, would you?"

A faint smile touched Charlie's lips. He avoided the question. "We better get you and Riley down to the doc. Those wounds need tending to. Besides, I've got to go tell Bonnie you two are okay. She's been mighty worried about you."

Chapter Sixteen

Tom stood leaning against the corral post and watched Tap and the men ride from the ranch. The plains lay wide and beige-white, shimmering in the early morning sunlight. The mountains, miles away in the distance rose like purple shadows, hiding their heads against the vast bosom of the sky.

As the riders became small, dark spots in the distance he turned and walked slowly toward the house. His wounds were healing and it felt good to be on his feet and moving around again.

His wild and reckless years now seemed to him to be far behind, in another life, another world. He had come to like the more peaceful strain of living though it too had been filled with gunsmoke, blood, and death.

He glanced again at Charlie's shaggy mustang standing in the corral with its ears pricked and watching his slow movements. He grinned to himself as he thought about Charlie. The thoughts of his little brother made his eyes grow softer. It had been worth the money he had paid for the strawberry roan to see the happy smile on Charlie's face when he gave it to him yesterday. Suddenly he shook his head as if to drive away these sensitive thoughts. 'Thinking like some ole granny' he muttered to himself.

The door opened and Bonnie stepped out on the porch. She was dressed in a blue calico dress with her long, auburn hair falling loosely over her shoulders. She presented a striking picture.

"Good morning, Tom. Looks like everyone is on the mend and feeling better. I can hardly remember the time when someone wasn't recovering from a gunshot or something. I'm glad the range has become peaceful and settled down."

"I've been giving that a lot of thought, Ms. Drake. Doggone if it don't seem kind of strange."

"Come on over and have a seat. I'll get us some coffee."

"Much obliged. Don't mind if I do sit a spell. I've been meaning to speak to you about something. It's been bothering me for quite some time." Tom removed his hat and sat down, running his fingers through his thick, curly shock of hair. The faint breeze felt good on his face.

Bonnie returned with the coffee and sat down beside him. "Well, Tom, it's been almost seven weeks since you were in jail and I made a deal with you. You've got ten months left."

"Yeah, I remember, Ms. Drake. You drove a hard bargain. Caught me in a tight spot."

"You may call me Bonnie if you like. Ms. Drake makes me feel kind of old."

"Okay, Bonnie. I like that better anyway. By the way, where's Charlie? I haven't seen him all morning."

"I gave him the day off. He's in his room dressing now. I thought the three of us might ride into town together if you don't mind."

"Don't mind at all. I was wanting to see Riley before he left town."

The sound of voices on the porch arrested Charlie's attention. This was the first time he had known of Tom and Bonnie engaging in a private conversation. He slipped out the back door and walked around the house until he came to the corner near the porch. He didn't like to think of himself as an evesdropper but to satisfy his curiosity he made allowances for this one time.

"Have you ever thought about settling down, Tom? I mean, on a ranch of your own?" There was a slight quiver in Bonnie's voice.

"I reckon I have at times. I guess a man ought to plant his roots someplace."

"Have you ever had anyone with whom you wanted to share your life with? Surely you have had a girl back down the road somewhere."

Tom avoided looking in her direction. "Can't rightly say there has ever been any particular girl in my life. The way I've knocked around the only things special in my life have been a straight shooting gun and a fast horse."

"There's a place for you here. I like having you close around."

Tom felt the red creeping up his neck and spreading to his face. He knew he was in a dangerous position but he liked this beautiful woman with the warm, gentle voice. "Well, our deal will keep me here for a year. I wouldn't welch on you."

"I'm not talking about our deal. If that

were the only reason you had for staying I'd release you from it."

Tom set his coffee cup on the floor and looked at her. "The truth is, Bonnie, I'd like to stay. I like being close around you. I've never had feelings for anyone like I do for you. But I've got the reputation of being a gunfighter and I've been a rustler. What woman would want such a man as that?"

"I would, Tom."

Tom's eyes widened and he stared at her in unbelief. "Do you really know what you're saying?"

"Yes, I know what I'm saying."

"Besides, there's something else I have to tell you. About an incident that occurred a couple of months ago in Amarillo."

"There's no need to say it. I've already guessed it. If it hadn't been you, then it would have been someone else. Luke couldn't handle his drinking."

"Doggone it, Bonnie! I'm going to say what's been on my mind for a spell. I've wanted to say it a dozen times but I couldn't get up enough courage."

"What on earth is it?"

Tom squirmed around on his chair. "It's a thing that's hard to just spit out."

Little Charlie

"Yes." Bonnie smiled as she watched Tom struggling helplessly.

"I… I can't sleep good at night for thinking about it."

"Good heavens! What is it?"

"I, uh… I love you, Bonnie."

Bonnie set her cup on the floor and rose from her chair. She leaned over Tom, placing her face within inches of his. "Those are the most beautiful words I've ever had spoken to me. And you know something else?"

"What's that?"

"I love you too, Tom Matthews!" She placed her lips against his for a long moment.

Tom held her hands in his and a worried expression covered his face. "You won't mention any of this to Charlie, will you?"

"Don't mention it to Charlie! Why shouldn't we tell him about it and that we intend to get married?"

"Ah, Bonnie, he thinks I'm a big, tough hombre of some kind. If he finds out about this he will think I'm getting soft and all."

Bonnie began giggling. As she continued to laugh, Tom's face grew red.

Neither one heard the low chuckling behind the corner of the house as Charlie cupped his hands over his mouth and laughed with Bonnie.

"See there! You're laughing at me yourself."

"Oh, Tom, you big sweetheart. I'm not laughing at you. I'm laughing because I love you and what you are. I think Charlie feels the same way I do."

"That brings to mind another thing. What are we gonna do about Charlie? I mean, how do you feel about him living with us and all?"

At these words Charlie held his breath. He strained his ears so as not to miss a word.

"Why, I love Charlie. After all, had it not been for him you and I would never have gotten together. I've already made plans for him. We're going to make him the assistant ranch manager with me. How does that sound?"

"That's real kind of you, Bonnie. I'm sure Charlie will like that very much."

As these words filled Charlie's ears his freckles beamed and his face broke into a smile. 'Assistant ranch manager!' He kept repeating the words over and over to himself. His heart was pounding wildly as he ran back around the house and entered. He lifted his hand and brushed away the drops that were beginning to trickle down his cheeks. He'd never had anyone to love him like Tom and

Bonnie. With his smile getting bigger and bigger he settled his new hat down on his shock of red hair.

Tom pulled the wagon to a stop in front of Godwin's Hardware. He helped Bonnie from the seat and looked at Charlie. "You remember what I told you, okay?"

Charlie grinned. "Sure,

"Tom! Hey, Tom!"

Tom and Bonnie turned to see who was calling.

Forbes walked up. On his shirt front was pinned a sheriff's badge. "Howdy, folks. Good to see you all in town."

"Howdy, sheriff. Looks like a plumb peaceful town you got here." Tom looked over his shoulder. "Come over here, Charlie. I want Sheriff Forbes to meet the new assistant ranch manager of the Rocking D."

Forbes grinned as he shook Charlie's hand. "Doggone if you ain't coming up in the world, Charlie."

"Maybe you two should go into Godwin's together. Bonnie and I will be in later. Here's a list of what we need, Charlie. Have Mr. Godwin to load it in the wagon. Sheriff

Forbes can inform Godwin of your new status on the ranch."

Bert was busy behind the counter when Forbes and Charlie stepped inside. He spoke without looking up when he heard the door open and close. "Be right with you in a min…" He glanced up and saw Charlie.

Unconsciously, Bert's fingers closed around the handle of a hammer lying on the counter. "Charlie Matthews! You lit…"

"Hold on there, Bert! I'm with Charlie. I just wanted to inform you that he's a man of means now. Yessir, the Rocking D has a new assistant manager. Charlie Matthews is his name. If I were you I'd be right respectful to him. He may decide to take his business elsewhere."

"Assistant ranch manager! Charlie!" The words seemed to almost choke him as he stared at Charlie.

Charlie strode up to the counter and handed Bert the list of supplies. "I'd be much obliged if you would have this loaded in the wagon within the hour, Mr. Godwin. I'm a busy man and I need to get back to the ranch as soon as possible." As he turned to leave a voice stopped him.

"Young man, would you be so kind as to

get me that pan hanging up there? Here's a stool to stand on."

"Why, certainly, ma'am. I'll have that pan in your hand in a jiffy," said Charlie.

"No, Charlie! Please! Here, Mrs. Tibbs, let me get that for you." Bert hurried from around the counter. "I can't have my important customers doing these menial tasks that I should be doing."

They all turned at the sound of a low chuckle behind them and saw Riley at the door.

"Good to see you, Charlie. I hear you've been promoted out on the ranch. Congratulations!"

"Thanks, Riley. I was hoping to see you before you left."

"I'm on my way now. You take care of Tom and Bonnie, you hear? Well, Forbes, if you're ready we'll go get the prisoners. The stage will be pulling out in a few minutes."

As they turned to walk out they turned back quickly at the sound of a loud crash and looked toward the counter.

Bert was lying on the floor with pots and pans scattered all around him.

The back door opened and Mrs. Godwin rushed inside. When she saw Bert lying on the floor among the scattered articles she jerked a broom from the rack. "Bert Godwin! You clumsy clown! Look at what a mess you've made." She advanced upon him with the broom lifted high in her hands.

As Bert scrambled to his feet she brought the broom down against his backside. "Charlie, grab that shotgun and load it, will you?" She winked at Charlie.

"I'd be delighted, Mrs. Godwin." He looked at Bert with a twinkle of mischief in his eyes and reached for the shotgun.

End.

Little Charlie

Shadow

With the wolves closing in from behind, he fought against the panic that was overtaking him. There was a tearing sensation in his leg every time the horse's hooves hit the ground and rose again. He was slowly losing his hold on the travois.

Suddenly he slashed the rawhide rope that bound Shadow to the stretcher. He and the dog were left rolling on the snow as the horse stampeded on up the bottoms.

For a moment after he came to a stop, he lay still. His head was spinning and his eyes would not focus. He heard the savage growls near him but could not see them.

Through half-blinded eyes he finally made out the dark form lying near him. It was Shadow. The coat had been torn from his body and he lay still, maybe lifeless. He blinked his eyes and shook his head. The dizziness began to wane. It was none too soon for circling around him and the dog were seven wolves, their vicious snarls and growls rising louder.

Moss hovered over the body of Shadow. With his knife in his hand, he yelled at the beasts preparing to attack. He had reached for his gun but his belt had been torn from his waist by the dragging over the snow."

Little Charlie

The Long Journey Home

There was a large oak tree standing about ten feet below me and would further divert the Indian's view of Quatie and Josh. I leaped for the tree. As suddenly as I jumped from behind the hickory tree toward the oak, the Indian sprang from his hiding place and with a savage whine hurled his hatchet tomahawk.

I was running with my head leaning forward and just reaching the oak tree when the hatchet struck the tree, not three inches from my head, the blade burying itself deeply into the tree. If he had aimed at the main part of my body, I would have been a goner, for the tomahawk would have split my side.

As soon as the tomahawk had left his hand, the Indian lunged for me, his hunting knife held low. I met his rush, swinging the shotgun with a hard blow that missed his head but collided with his shoulder. I saw his face wince in momentary pain, then he began circling me, wanting to get above me and place me at a disadvantage. I circled with him, keeping him downhill.

He was about my height and heavy with muscle in his broad shoulders and deep chest. The red, dark purple, and yellow paint covered most of his copper face. His gleaming eyes were filled with the lust to kill.

Out of the corner of my eye I saw Josh untying Quatie's hands and feet.

The Indian lunged at me again, slashing with his knife. The blade caught my forearm, cutting through my shirt and leaving a shallow trail of blood. Had I not stepped quickly back the sweeping blow would have opened up my stomach. As it was, my foot slipped and I fell backwards. The Indian leaped, his knife held high and just before he landed on me to drive the knife through my chest, I swung the shotgun with all my strength, hitting the wrist that held the knife. There was a loud popping sound as the bone snapped and his eyes filled with both pain and fear. The knife had gone sailing through the air downhill.

We both leaped to our feet. The Indian glanced around, hoping to see his knife but it was nowhere in sight. He began slowing backing away. When he had put fifteen feet between us he looked up and shook his head.

"Josh," I yelled.

The transformation had already begun when the knife hurled from Josh's hand struck the Indian high on his right arm, cutting through the muscle and extending through the other side. The transformation concluded and the Great Horned owl started to spread its wings to take flight, but its right wing collapsed, preventing it. It floundered helplessly on the ground, rolling downhill with Josh quickly pursuing it.

As I walked over to stand beside Quatie, we heard a loud shrieking sound far below us and then silence.

"Bidziil," said Quatie. "He will bother us no more."

Little Charlie

The Savage Land

Santiago Hernandez knew the man he was facing. He had avoided the Texan-bred rancher and swung wide of his ranch in his rustling exploits, remembering the first and only brush he had had with him. And the man who sat by his side was cut from the same cloth. Suddenly he wished he had a dozen more men with him.

Santiago's mouth opened and spread into a wide smile, revealing white, gleaming teeth. "Ah, senor Dawson, what a surprise. Get down...get down and have a drink with us." He laughed loudly.

"I'm gonna have a drink in a little bit, Santiago. But I've got some business to take care of first."

"What kind of business, senor? You are far away from your rancho."

Clay chuckled. "We had some mules and horses to stray away last night." He nodded toward the stolen herd. "I see they ended up here. I'm much obliged to you for holding them until we got here."

Santiago burst into a spasm of laughter. "But

senor Dawson, these are not your mules and horses. As you can see...there are no Half Moon brands on them."

"Yeah, I can see," replied Clay. "They're all Slash M brands. I'm picking them up for my friend Leonardo."

A shocked expression spread over Santiago's dark face. Clay could see he was genuinely surprised.

"But Leonardo...he is dead. He has not been seen in two...maybe three weeks now."

"No, he's not dead and even if he was, this stock still belongs to his ranch."

Santiago shrugged his shoulders. Even though a wide grin was still on his face, his hand moved a little closer to his gun. "Perhaps I might sell the mules and horses. You are a reasonable man, senor Clay. Name me a price you are willing to pay."

"Here's the deal, Santiago," said Clay in a casual voice. "If you and your men trail the herd back to the Morales' ranch, it will cost you only a hundred dollars."

"You mean for me to pay you one hundred dollars?"

"That's right. It took sixteen men off their jobs to come after them."

A puzzled look filled Santiago's eyes. He

stole a nervous look back toward the summit of the slope. Suddenly he burst out in laughter again. "Sixteen men! But there are only four of you. Are you saying each one of your men is equal to four?"

Loud laughing broke out among the rustlers who were listening intently.

Santiago waved his arm around toward the rustlers. "See… my men…they like your joking."

"Well, what's its gonna be? You can pay the hundred up front," said Clay.

Santiago was still laughing. "A hundred, eh? How about this?" He grabbed for his gun.

Little Charlie

Dawson

Chad Larkin licked his dry lips as his ferret eyes searched the ground below him. Not twenty feet away lay the gun of the man who had tumbled down the hillside.

He knew his man was hit and he believed it to be a critical wound for he had been knocked from the saddle and landed hard on the ground. He must find him for the boss liked to see the bodies of the men they were after. Even if the bullet hadn't killed him, the hard fall and tumbling downhill might have.

The screaming of Ted Harbin had unnerved him for a little bit. Never had he seen such fear and pain-filled eyes. The bullet he had taken in the belly must have torn him up inside.

By the time he had reached Ted, he was on his knees and clutching his belly with both arms. He had stretched him out to examine the wound but when he saw it, he knew there was nothing to be done.

At Ted's bidding, he had leaned him up against a tree in a sitting position, promising Ted he wouldn't leave him. Ted's eyes had closed for a couple of minutes and Chad thought he might have died until he felt his neck for a pulse. It was there, shallow but he was still breathing.

When Ted had opened his eyes again, he asked for water. Chad had looked around to see their horses standing fifty feet away, their heads high and staring in their direction. He went for a canteen.

He had reached the horses when he heard Ted scream. He turned and raced back, forgetting the water. It was a loud, high-pitched scream and had barely died when Chad leaped to the ground beside him.

Ted's eyes appeared as two yellow flames as he stared at Chad.

"A man…man." The brightness in his eyes faded and his eyes rolled around loosely in their sockets.

"A man? What man?" Chad had asked. He lifted Ted's sagging head and stared into his eyes. "Ted! What man?"

Ted's face tightened and he clutched his belly tighter. "Can't…stand…pain." He groaned loudly as his face turned darker. "Finish…it…Chad. Can't stand…it!"

It had been a hard thing to do. He had drawn his gun and leveled it at Ted's heart and turned his head when he pulled the trigger.

Chad continued searching the ground through watchful, careful eyes. The man was somewhere close. He could feel it.

There was a sudden drop of the ground forty feet below where he stood. Directly below the drop was an area covering some twenty feet that could not be seen. It was that area that filled his eyes with caution. The body could be lying there dead as a doornail, yet, it might not be and Chad Larkin was a man who disliked taking chances.

After a few minutes and seeing no movement, no sign of the body, Chad stepped out, but in a direction that circled around the drop-off. He moved slowly, his gun ready and his eyes watchful.

He was level with the place below the drop-off when he suddenly hunkered down behind the trunk of a tree. His eyes widened at sight of the dark cave mouth. On the ground and just in front of it he saw the portion of a man's arm and hand. As he watched, the arm and hand slowly disappeared from sight.

Chad leaped from behind the tree, his gun ready for firing. He caught the sudden movement from the corner of his eye causing him to spin sideways and he fired. Below him, not over a hundred feet away, a man had

Little Charlie

stepped out from behind a tree.

Deathsong

He rode at a shambling trot, the only sounds being the creaking saddle and the even rhythm of the horse's hooves. He had decided to spend a couple of nights in town. The isolation at the ranch was wearing on his nerves.

He had been listening to the added sound for two full minutes before it registered in his brain. Another horse had fallen in behind him, its hoofbeats blending in with his. Above the tatoo of the horses' hooves rose a low, faint whistling.

His first impulse was to feed the spurs to his horse. He overcame the sensation and rode on, refusing to look behind him.

The whistling became louder as the horse behind began drawing closer. When he judged the distance to be no more than twenty feet, he spoke. "Thought maybe you weren't coming, Wade. Decided to ride into town and have a drink. You want to join me for one?"

"Don't reckon I'd care to, Tom. I prefer drinking with friends." His voice was calm and gentle.

Tom pulled his horse to a halt and rested both hands on the saddlehorn. He watched the small shadow on the ground as it swung into a slow moving circle. As he lifted his eyes and glanced at the large, black bird, it dropped lower in the air.

"Reckon you've come to settle up, Wade. Not much use in talking. What's been done is done."

"Yeah, nothing can change that," replied Wade. He had stopped his horse when Wade pulled up. "I didn't take you for the kind of man you are, Tom. I thought you were my friend." His voice held a slight trace of regret.

Slowly Tom turned his horse to face him. There was no fear in him, just a tired, weary feeling. As he looked at Wade he recalled how he had saved his life. He shrugged his shoulders. "Kind of wish things had turned out different."

"Like maybe me being burned to ashes in the fire, uh? I can imagine you would have liked that much better." His voice remained the same, low and gentle. Only his eyes changed. The yellow flared up in them revealing the deep, hot passion that burned in his heart.

Tom's hand darted to his gun. It was out of the holster and swinging to a firing position when Wade's gun exploded and the bullet tore through his chest. It entered his left shirt pocket and pierced the sack of Bull-Durham, burning its way through the flesh and the heart of Tom.

A faint smile passed over Tom's lips as he toppled from his saddle. He was dead before he hit the ground.

Wade dismounted and looked down at the body. The smile had frozen on Tom's face. He lifted the body and draped it over the saddle. After tying it in place he mounted again and led the horse toward town.

Three of the men were now dead. That left only two, Bob Savage and Charlie Stroupe. They had slipped Mabel and Mary Jane away from the ranch before he arrived.

He rode on toward town through the stillness of the waning evening. When the buildings of the town loomed into sight, he stopped. After tying the reins of Tom's horse to the saddlehorn he slapped it hard on the rump in the direction of town.

For a long minute he sat his saddle and watched as the horse carried the dead body toward town.

Turning his horse's head, he pointed it back toward the ranch and began to whistle.

The bird overhead had been joined by two of his friends. They had started climbing higher in the sky, every circle making them smaller. They had watched as the horse carried the dead body toward town but had fallen in overhead of the rider heading in the opposite direction. They decided to stick with him. His trail promised to be more rewarding.

Little Charlie

Little Charlie

Little Charlie

Made in the USA
Monee, IL
22 January 2026

42057311R00132